I was in Greg's office when the e-mail came that would change everything.

I clicked to open it, and a picture began to download. I swallowed, and put a hand to my chest, trying to calm the rapid beats of my heart. I closed my eyes—*please, God*—but when I opened them, the picture was still there.

"Lilly? You okay?" Greg said.

"Fine," I said. My voice was whispery and it cracked. *This is a dream. If I close my laptop, the picture will go away.* I tried it. But the picture was still there.

"Something's the matter, I can tell." He came toward me, and in that instant I wanted to melt into his arms. I wanted him to make everything okay. He touched my face. "What is it? A bad e-mail? Something from school?"

I shook my head. "No." At least that wasn't a lie. It was definitely not something from school.

Books by Linda Hall

Love Inspired Suspense

Shadows in the Mirror #71
Shadows at the Window #107

LINDA HALL

When people ask award-winning author Linda Hall when it was that she got the "bug" for writing, she answers that she was probably in fact born with a pencil in her hand. Linda has always loved reading and would read far into the night, way past when she was supposed to turn her lights out. She still enjoys reading and probably reads a novel a week.

She also loved to write, and drove her childhood friends crazy wanting to spend summer afternoons making up group stories. She's carried that love into adulthood with twelve novels.

Linda has been married for thirty-five years to a wonderful and supportive husband who reads everything she writes and who is always her first editor. The Halls have two children and three grandchildren.

Growing up in New Jersey, her love of the ocean was nurtured during many trips to the shore. When she's not writing, she and her husband enjoy sailing the St. John River system and the coast of Maine in their 28-foot sailboat, *Gypsy Rover II.*

Linda loves to hear from her readers and can be contacted at Linda@writerhall.com. She invites her readers to her Web site, which includes her blog and pictures of her sailboat: http://writerhall.com.

Shadows at the Window

LINDA HALL

Steeple
Hill®

Published by Steeple Hill Books™

STEEPLE HILL BOOKS

Steeple
Hill®

ISBN-13: 978-0-373-44297-3
ISBN-10:   0-373-44297-1

SHADOWS AT THE WINDOW

www.SteepleHill.com

Printed in U.S.A.

Therefore, if anyone is in Christ, he is a new creation; the old has gone, the new has come!
—2 *Corinthians* 5:17

To Rik

ONE

I was in my boyfriend Greg's office when the e-mail came that would change everything. Greg is the youth pastor at the church I've been attending for seven years. My apartment building is just two doors away, so it's easy for me to pop over. Of course, that's something I do a lot. Any excuse is a good excuse for a visit.

Nothing seemed out of the ordinary that day. I traipsed into the church carrying my backpack, my classical guitar and a cardboard tray containing four coffees, plus a small bag of doughnut holes, which I had to hold in my teeth. There wasn't a whole lot of time for a visit and a chat. I had a guitar student at the music store where I work part-time, plus a music class of my own at the college in the afternoon.

Even though I was visiting Greg, I knew better than to bring coffee for just the two of us. There would probably be at least two more bodies in the church this morning. Brenda, the church secretary, would be there, along with Dave, the senior pastor. Paige, the music director, works part-time so I wasn't sure she'd be there but I was hoping she would. I had written a few of the worship songs that we sang in church and was having difficulty resolving the last verse of a new song—I was eager for her input. For the past seven years, Paige has been my music mentor. She's also been my good friend. She and her husband Henry are those rare people who you could call at three in the morning when bad news comes. Their daughter Sara is taking classical guitar lessons from me. I like her a lot.

I managed to push open the church door with my shoulder without spilling the coffee and found a gaping hole in the floor. The entire place was strung with caution tape. I'd have to walk through the basement, get lost and try to find my way up through narrow hallways back to the office area. The old building was undergoing a massive facelift. It was either that or tear it down. Since it's a heritage building, the church really had no option but to renovate.

This past summer the exterior was fully refurbished, complete with new copper turrets. And now that it was getting cooler, the inside was being torn out and rebuilt.

"I smell coffee," Brenda said, poking her head out of her office and talking to me over the yellow tape and the hole in the floor.

I dropped the doughnuts on top of the coffees and answered her.

"Yeah, but can I get there from here? Can I jump over?"

She shook her head. "I wouldn't even try it. They're taking up the floorboards and we've been warned that it's dangerous. I don't want you falling down two floors. Do you know the way through the basement?"

"Barely," I said. "I always get lost down there." It's full of bugs, too, I wanted to add, but didn't. "You guys need to put up a detour sign," I joked.

"Don't laugh. Dave wants me to do just that. Wait there. I'll come around and get you. Greg's on the phone or he would."

"Thanks." I leaned against the wall, laid my guitar case on the floor, and rested the tray of coffees and the doughnuts on top of it. Paint-splattered workmen chatted among themselves as they hammered and sawed. I heard the far-off sound of drills, saws and other equipment. Dust was everywhere. With both hands I pulled my hair out of my eyes and shoved it behind my ears. It was frizzing more than usual in the wet weather we'd been having. As I waited, I hummed a new praise song we'd sung here a week ago.

It seemed like five minutes before Brenda reappeared and picked up the bag of doughnut holes and the tray of coffees, saying, "How nice." I followed her down the main staircase to the basement, along an uneven cement corridor flanked on either side by tiny, dusty rooms which looked as though they were used for storage. I am seldom down in the bowels of the church—it's not a particularly appetizing place. I brushed cobwebs out of my hair as we made our way through the narrow hallways.

She said, "Soon this'll be torn up, too. They're planning to open up this whole area, tear out every single wall you see and put in bigger classrooms."

"That'll be nice."

"How's school?"

"It's great. I didn't think I'd like it, but I'm settling in. It's been more than ten years since I've been in school, but I'm right back in the routine."

"You'll do fine," Brenda said.

We went up a set of skinny, creaky steps—the wood was shiny, worn down by a century of footsteps—and into yet another passage that led into the brightness of the wide church hallway, which housed the offices. I gave Brenda two coffees and some of the doughnut holes, and took the rest to Greg's office.

He was still on the phone, leaning against his bookshelf. I set my offerings on his desk. He smiled when he saw me. His grin widened when he saw the doughnut holes.

I realized that he was standing because the two chairs in his office were entirely covered with books, papers, CDs, DVDs, leaflets and odd bits of things. His entire office was in disarray. I moved one pile from a chair onto the floor as Greg said, "That would be fine. Yes, that's doable…"

I looked at his face, at the crinkles around the edges of his light blue eyes, the way he absently brushed his hands through his messy dark-blond hair. He was wearing faded jeans and a dark blue golf shirt with a little sailboat embossed on the pocket. To most people, Greg seemed like one of those big, affable teddy-bear kind of guys. Very few people know that a lot of pain is hidden behind that happy-go-lucky exterior. Sometimes it frightens me, the depth of pain both of us have come through to get to a point where we are almost ready to commit to each other. But we did, and we are, and sometimes I have to pinch myself for my good fortune and God's blessings. Life is good.

"Hey, gorgeous," was the first thing he said when he hung up the phone.

"Gorgeous? I like that!"

"You think I was talking about you?" He reached for me, gave me a quick kiss. "I was talking about the coffee."

With both hands he managed to lift a three-foot pile of books from the other chair, balancing them under his chin before he placed them on the floor. A small, rectangular carpet covered with roads and villages lay on the floor beyond his desk. He's had this since he was a boy and can't part with it—he says that when the stresses of the ministry get to be too much for him, he can push his favorite Matchbox cars around the avenues and lanes on his carpet. I've never actually seen him do this, though.

He flipped up the plastic tab on a coffee and inhaled the aroma. "Nectar of the gods," he said. "They're going to have this in Heaven."

I extracted my laptop from my backpack, took a sip of my coffee and looked around. "So, when did the hurricane hit?"

"Organizing," was his reply. Munching on a doughnut hole, he said, "They've told me they're going to tear down this wall next week, so I really have no choice but to go through my books. Get rid of some stuff. Organize."

"Tear out that wall? What's on the other side?"

"A lounge that nobody uses. And then, supposedly,

they're going to enlarge this little cubby hole of an office for me—more space, new floors, the works."

On top of one haphazard mound, his laptop perched precariously; his wastebasket overflowed with papers and other bits of trash. I looked down and saw a whole file folder full of Christmas cards he'd received. Christmas cards? It was September!

On the floor were more stacks of books and a variety of newspapers and magazines. I picked up one. It was from three years ago. "Hey," I said. "I know a doctor's office you could take these to."

"Funny," was his comment. "My bookshelves are overloaded."

"Ya think?" My laptop had booted up. I was about to check my e-mail on the church's Wi-Fi when he said, "Cinni called."

I looked up. "Yeah?"

"She and Sara are doing up some sort of spreadsheet."

"Wow. They're really working hard."

"They want to show it to us," he said.

We were in the middle of the fall youth fund-raising clean up. As the youth pastor's girlfriend, my arm had been twisted into heading the committee, which consisted of Paige and Henry's daughter Sara, and Sara's friend Cinni. The money we were raising was going to purchase books for an African school.

My e-mail began to download. So much spam. I looked up at Greg and smiled. He was looking at me intently, so intently. We didn't say anything for a minute. Sometimes when I'm around Greg, I'm nervous that this whole wonderful new life of mine is going to come crashing down.

"What?" I asked, still smiling.

"I'm just thinking about tonight."

Tonight. I hugged my knees. "I could never forget that."

It was our six-month anniversary. We would be going to the same restaurant we went to on our first date, Primo's Pizza. I know, I know, some would say it's just a pizza joint, but the place—in all its laid-back splendor—holds special memories for us. Plus, they make the best pizza in all of Boston.

And then Greg started telling me about a youth conference he was going to go to in a couple of weeks and how he wanted to get his office cleaned up and ready before he left. My e-mails downloaded as I listened. Wading through spam these days is a full-time job. Delete. Delete. Delete. It seemed to be the only key I was pressing.

When it came—that e-mail that would changes everything—I almost deleted it, too. In retrospect, maybe I should have.

It was from a Hotmail account and the subject line read, "TO YOU, LCJ."

My initials: L.C.J. Lilly Carolynne Johnson. Lilly spelled with two Ls instead of one. My mother's doing—my mother who wanted me to be different than the flower, my mother whom I hadn't seen in two years and hardly ever heard from. I shoved that thought away. I was too happy with Greg to let it interfere.

I clicked to open the e-mail and a picture began to download on my screen.

"...And so then I'm thinking, why can't we clean the houses of anyone who asks? I mean, we've got people coming out of the woodwork these days. It doesn't have to just be church people. That's what I told Dave. And Cinni."

Greg is a great talker. I think it's because he's a pastor and counsels youth, and also delivers sermons— he has to be a talker. He was pulling books from his bookshelf while he chatted on and on, as much to himself as to me.

I was watching the picture download onto my screen. I felt cemented to my chair. Occasionally, I managed a nod just to show that I was listening. "...And so I've got that to deal with on top of this whole church-building thing." He picked up a thick book. "I should just get rid of this commentary. I'll check with Dave. Maybe he could use it the whole set. These belonged to my dad, actually. That's how old they are." Greg's dad had been a minister before him.

I could barely make out the meaning of the words he was saying to me. The picture was now open on my screen. I swallowed, put a hand to my chest, trying to quell the rapid beats of my heart. All that I said before about pinching myself for God's blessing? I take it all back. This picture could shatter that dream like a window besieged by baseballs.

I closed my eyes—*please, God*—but when I opened them, the picture was still there. The image was grainy and obviously had been uploaded from another source. The young woman on my screen was bone thin and her hair hung to her shoulders, straight and black. She looked tough, this girl, with her blue lipstick and dark-rimmed eyes. She wore a leather bustier, a skirt which ended midthigh, and boots. And chains. Lots of chains. She was the kind of girl you'd expect to have tattoos and multiple piercings, the kind you would not want your son to date.

Greg must've seen something in my eyes because he stopped what he was doing and said, "Lilly? You okay?"

"Fine." My voice was whispery and it cracked. I coughed and took a few deep breaths. *This is a dream. If I close my laptop, the picture will go away.* I tried it. But when I opened it again, the picture was still there.

I quickly shut down my computer and stuffed it into my backpack, telling Greg I had to leave. Right now. I looked at my watch for effect. I'd forgotten how late it was getting, I told him. I stood and made for the door.

Greg looked surprised, "Lilly?"

"Yes?"

"Something's the matter, I can tell." He came toward me, and in that instant, I wanted to melt into his arms and never leave that safe and warm place. I wanted him to make everything okay. I wanted to forget that the girl on my computer screen had ever existed.

A tear winked at the corner of my eye. I blinked rapidly. Greg touched my face. "What is it? A bad e-mail? Something from school?"

I shook my head. "No." That wasn't a lie. It wasn't from school. It was definitely *not* something from school.

He took my hand, led me back to his desk. "Come here, babe. Let me show you something that'll cheer you up. I almost forgot. You have to look at this before you go."

I followed him to the desk like a puppy dog. What else could I do? He opened his laptop, clicked through a few links and then said, "Ta da!" He turned the screen to face me.

For one horrid moment I thought he was going to show me the photo of the girl. He didn't. It was our church's brand-new Web site and there was a picture of me, front and center.

"The world's most beautiful singer. In all her splendor," he said.

I blinked. There I was, holding a microphone in one hand, raising my other hand toward the congregation. The lights had picked up the glints in my strawberry-blond hair. My skin was so pale, I looked like a ghost.

I said, "Is this new? I didn't know I was on the Web."

Greg nodded. "Stuart's done an amazing job. You remember that sorry-looking old thing we called a Web site? It's gone now. This is our new, professional Web site—it even has pictures of the youth group. You'll get a kick out of this one." For the next few minutes we clicked through the various links. "Stuart's even arranged it so that there's a blog. It's mostly for the youth group, but anyone can post if they want to."

"Stuart did this?"

"Yep."

I always felt a bit unnerved around Stuart—the church's projectionist-slash-soundman-slash-resident sci-fi expert, and now apparently, slash-webmaster. He works in the projectionist booth here in the church and is always in black: black T-shirts, black jeans, black boots.

A few years ago, before Greg moved here, Stuart and I went out. Once. We went to a movie, some classic sci-fi film that he kept raving over. The whole thing bored me to pieces with its continual chase scenes, and aliens oozing green and killing people by breathing on them.

Later over coffee, he had seemed almost angry when I said it wasn't really my thing.

"But it's a classic!"

Since then, our relationship has been cordial, but that's it. There are times, though, when I find him gazing at me with those intense, dark eyes and I have to look away. So, he put me on the Web site, did he?

"A blog. Cool," I said, without enthusiasm, attempting a cheerfulness I didn't feel. "Well," I said, "time for me to get going."

Greg walked me down the back stairs, through the basement with its cobwebby rooms and out the front door of the church, holding my hand the whole time. Even though we were in front of the church, and it was the middle of the day, and there were construction workers all around, he kissed me for a long time. Then he said quietly, "I know things have been hard for you, Lilly. I know the things you've gone through, but I just want you to know that everything is going to be different now. You're with me. And with God. I love you, Lilly."

When he left, I caught my reflection in the window of the front door of the church. My face looked pale and watery in the glass, like it would melt.

I knew that girl in the picture. I knew her all too well.

TWO

I somehow managed to get through my work at the music store and my guitar lesson with my student Irma who, like she did every week, arrived early with foil-wrapped treats from her kitchen. Today, almond brownies. When she handed them to me she said, "You're not as happy as I'd thought you'd be. Isn't tonight a special night for you?"

I blinked. Had I told positively everyone?

"I'm fine," I said. "Let's have a listen to that chord progression you're working on."

"I practiced every day," she said.

I'm convinced Irma spends whole days practicing the guitar her late husband used to play in a country band. It's a beat-up Martin with a fantastic sound.

After the lesson, I put my head inside a cheerful bubble and finished the day. I attended my afternoon music-history class and made myself smile a lot. But later in the practice room, I couldn't get my fingers to obey my brain's commands on the piano. And as the clock moved steadily toward evening, I was slowly coming undone. I gave up on Beethoven and pulled out the notebook where I'd jotted down the lyrics to my unfinished worship song. I took my classical guitar out of the case and began. But as I went through the nowfamiliar melody, I paused midphrase. What did I think I was doing? How could I possibly think I could write worship songs to God? I tried to resolve the chords, but my fingers refused to find the final notes in the sequence.

For several minutes, I forced myself to work on it. I hit wrong strings and played chords that sounded like my life today—jarring, off key and dissonant.

I jutted out my bottom lip, blew my bangs out of my eyes and tried again, but no matter how much I pursued that piece, I could not finish it. I looked down at my trembling hands as if they belonged to someone else.

Why was someone sending me a picture of that girl? Why, when everything was just beginning to get good again? I sighed loudly. *I can't go out with him tonight. I can't see Greg.*

I had the feeling that Greg was going to ask me to marry him tonight. All the signs were there. Even Bridget, my roommate and best friend, had heard things. A few weeks ago, he'd taken both my hands, looked me in the eyes and said, "Two weeks. The night of our anniversary, we'll go out. I've got it all planned. Don't let *anything* interfere."

I had looked into the depths of his blue eyes and said, "I don't intend to."

And why would I? Greg and I been going out pretty much exclusively for six months. I was twenty-nine, he was thirty. We were madly in love. So what were we waiting for?

I had already started picking out wedding colors. If he asked me tonight, we could be married in the spring. I'd even bought a *Brides* magazine—one—which I'd shoved into my top dresser drawer. I brought it out every once in a while to flip through it and dream, but it always made me feel a little like an impostor. I just couldn't believe that could be mine. And now I knew it wouldn't be.

I placed my guitar back in the case and closed it. I couldn't marry Greg Whitten. I couldn't be with him. We would have to break up. I sat there. I listened. Through the muffled walls, I could hear the other students practicing. Somebody was playing something darkly discordant, another was working on a classic Beatles tune, and still another was playing a blues number. I smiled. That was probably my new class-mate Neil Stoner. A pale complected, serious young man, he plays both piano and cello—he transferred this year from a school out west. Neil and I—plus two bright-eyed sophomores named Tiff and Lora—were working on a music-history project. Sometimes I felt like a big sister to all of them.

Since I'd seen that picture on my computer screen, I'd thought about it a million times. It occurred to me that I could ask Stuart—he might have an idea how to find out where the e-mail had come from. I knew there were ways to do that but I didn't know how. If anyone would know, Stuart would.

I dismissed that idea as soon as it came to me. I

didn't need Stuart nosing around in my business. Earlier, I'd Googled the e-mail address, but came up with nothing. I knew enough to realize that anybody in the whole world, good guy or bad guy, could sign up for a Hotmail account. And then get rid of it just as quickly. It could be someone clear on the other side of the world—or it could be someone living right next door. That thought chilled me as I looked at the closed door of my practice room. Was I vulnerable in here? Was I vulnerable everywhere?

I thought about Greg. My love was probably making plans for tonight, maybe even getting flowers. Greg is very romantic. I shut my eyes, bent my head and leaned my cheek against the cool white piano keys. Suddenly I was remembering a man from a very long time ago who wasn't so romantic.

"Stop it, please! You're hurting me!"

"If you and Moira would listen to me for once instead of always trying to fight me on everything, I wouldn't have to keep you in line like this."

I closed my eyes, trying to quash those thoughts, but they simmered on the surface. *Stop it,* I told myself. *Think about good things, about pleasant things.* Doesn't the Bible encourage this, after all? I'd been trying to live by its precepts since I'd become a Christian seven years ago.

So why should this happen now? It just wasn't fair.

A tear fell onto the piano keys. I put my music books back into my bag, got out my cell phone and, before I could change my mind, called Greg at his home, a place I hoped he wouldn't be. The phone rang once and I had a horrible feeling that he might answer it. What if he'd gone home early? I was counting on him *not* answering. It rang twice. I held my breath. Three times and I began to relax. On the fourth ring it went to the machine, and I said as pleasantly as I could, "Greg? It's me. Sorry I missed you." I coughed a bit for effect. "I'm so sorry, but I'm going to have to cancel tonight. I know, I know, but I am just so totally sick. I don't know what's come over me, but you really do *not* want to be around me tonight. You might catch it. I'm surprised I can even talk this long on the phone without running to the bathroom. It came on me so suddenly. So, hey, I'll talk to you tomorrow. We'll reschedule." I hung up and very carefully and deliberately turned off my cell phone. Then I bent my head into my hands. I'd just told another lie in a long string of lies to the person I wanted to spent the rest of my life with.

When I got home to my apartment, I went into my room, and closed the door. I pulled my two big suitcases out from under my bed and haphazardly began stuffing clothes and books inside. When one suitcase was filled with my music books and composition papers, it became obvious that I couldn't take everything. But when I got to where I was going, wherever that was, I wouldn't be able to send for my stuff. Because I would have disappeared. Like I had eight years ago. Except I hadn't, had I?

My mistake, I thought, as I crammed in T-shirts and jeans and socks and sweaters, was in ever thinking that I could have a normal life—get married, have children, go to church and pick out china patterns— like a regular person.

If I got in my car right now, I could miss rush hour maybe. I looked out my window to the street three stories below. Bridget and I live on a semi-busy avenue lined with old brownstones like ours. It's also a pedestrian street with lots of ancient trees and people who walk dogs or jog or push baby carriages along the cement sidewalk. The church spire towers on the left, and I confess to often sitting right here, just to catch a glimpse of my beloved. I sat at the window and cried for all that I was about to lose.

And this is the way Bridget found me an hour later, sitting on my bed, clutching a book of poems that Greg had bought me, crying. I quickly dried my eyes on the ends of my sleeves and said, "What are you doing home so early?"

"Oh, Lilly!" She dropped the high heels she'd been holding and raced to my side. "You look so sick! Greg called me and told me you guys aren't going out tonight. Do you want me to stay home with you? Was it something you ate? Why don't I make some of my chicken soup?" She sat beside me, placed her perfectly manicured fingers on my forehead and looked at me sadly. Then she noticed the mess on my bed. "What's all this?"

If there is another person I didn't want to lie to, it's Bridget, but again, I didn't think I had a choice. We've shared this apartment for four years, and I value her wisdom and her friendship more than I can say. I could never lie to her and yet—and yet—I had and I would continue to do so.

I said, "I thought maybe of going home...I don't know."

"Are you that sick, Lilly?" Her eyes were wide as she sat beside me in her mauve designer suit. She pulled her stockinged feet up underneath her. Bridget works in a downtown Boston office. The first thing she does when she walks in the door from work is pull off her heels and groan about sore feet. She does this absolutely every day, even before she removes her coat.

Four years ago, when the rent on this place went up, it became apparent that with my music-store salary, I wasn't going to be able to afford a somewhat pricey, top-floor walkup on my own. It has basically three rooms: two bedrooms and a large living space which is a combination living and dining room with a kitchen nook in the back. It's a cute place, and even though it's as expensive as the sky, I didn't want to give it up. Plus, I love the location.

I let it be known around the church that I needed a roommate, and Bridget came and saw me. We've been best friends ever since. She seems so very sleek and so-phisticated, but she bakes tollhouse cookies on the weekend, knits socks for her nieces and nephews and knows the names of all our neighbors.

She was sitting beside me, a worried look on her face as she raised her flawlessly waxed eyebrows. Even at the end of the day, her auburn hair shimmered and fell into place like in a TV commercial.

"And you're going to need your music books there? A whole suitcase full of them?" She looked at me and then something seemed to register. "Oh Lilly, you really are sick, aren't you? Does Greg know? When did you find out?"

I put up my hand. I had to stop her. "No, no. I'm not dying. I'm okay. Well, sick, but okay. I'm just organizing. I was feeling a speck better, so I decided to organize."

"And you're going home?"

"I don't know. I'm just not thinking. I..." And then I began to cry deep, heaving sobs. I just couldn't stop myself.

Bridget hugged me. "I'll stay with you. I don't have to go to that stupid company dinner tonight. I'll call right now and cancel so I can be with you here. You shouldn't be alone."

"No, Bridget, you don't have to. Really. Don't miss your dinner on account of me."

"My dinner is nothing compared to the welfare of my best friend."

I looked down at my hands. Quietly, I said, "I lied to Greg. I'm not really sick, Bridget. I'm just afraid." I looked at her. "I can't go into it. It's complicated and has to do with a whole lot of stuff that happened to me before I came here, before I met Greg."

"But honey, everybody gets afraid. Everything is different for you now. You're a Christian. The past is in the past and you and Greg love each other."

I shook my head. Oh, if it were that simple. And as I looked up into the pretty face of my best friend, I thought about the pretty face of another best friend from a long time ago. Her name was Moira Peterson. At a time in my life when no one was my friend, we two clung to each other as if drowning.

THREE

I finally persuaded Bridget to go to her dinner when I told her I needed a bit of alone time to work through my thoughts and that I hoped she would understand. She left, but not without me promising that I'd call her on her cell if I needed her to come home. She'd come immediately, she said. Even if she were in the middle of a conversation with the owner of the company—even about a six-figure raise—she'd drop everything and skedaddle home. Bridget, who grew up in the country, freely uses words like skedaddle.

I couldn't wait for her to leave so I could cry in private, but when she did, I felt lonely, afraid and desperate. I was actually getting a stomachache. At this rate, I really would be throwing up. That thought gave me a peculiar sort of comfort. At least then I wouldn't be lying any more. I closed my eyes and snuggled down deep into the blankets on my bed.

I'd told Bridget I wanted to go home, when actually that was about the last place I wanted to go. Maybe I should go see Moira. I closed my eyes and it was ten years ago again—I was under a sheet in another house. It was muggy and hot, and mosquitoes whined at the broken screen. He had just left the room.

Mudd.

His name was Michael Binderson, but everybody called him Mudd.

My arm burned where he'd twisted it, and the back of my neck hurt from where he'd hit me. When I'd put my hand to that spot, there was blood. It had happened when I asked for my rightful share of the money. He told me I was no good, I'd messed up again, I was never good enough— Never. And then he raped me.

It happened all the time. When he was gone, I would lie under the hot sheets in the humid air and sob. Moira would hear me and come from the kitchen to hug me until my gasping tears settled.

"Mudd," I whispered his name in the darkness of my room in Boston. Mudd was the only person who would send me that picture. But he was dead. He'd been murdered eight years ago in a drug deal gone bad. Or so I thought.

I needed to leave. But where would I go? I couldn't go home. Once upon a time, a dozen years ago, I had a promising future but I walked out of my family's house and away from a college music scholarship. I thought I knew better than everybody; my parents, my guidance counselors, my music teachers. Five years ago, I reconnected with my parents, but we're not close. My mother still thinks I'm wasting my talents. She feels I should be studying classical guitar at a prestigious music school rather than at a local community college. And singing in a church? She really can't understand that one.

I couldn't go to Moira, either. Eight years was too long to wait to ask forgiveness.

My mouth felt dry. I reached over and checked that my cell phone was turned off. Bridget and I don't have a landline in our apartment so if my cell was turned off, no one could reach me. I sat up in bed.

Heaped around me were the clothes that I'd ripped out of my closet when I'd gotten home. On the floor, my music books and composition papers spilled out of one suitcase, and some of my clothes were piled in the other. My guitar was in its opened case. I got out of bed, picked it up and cautiously began to pluck out a melody and sing. I put it back. I couldn't get anything to sound right.

I glanced at my clock: 8:16. If I hadn't gotten that e-mail this morning I quite likely would be engaged by now. Maybe I'd be wearing a sparkly diamond and we'd be walking hand in hand on the sea wall, our favorite place. Or perhaps we'd be wandering through the mall picking out dishes and kitchen furniture.

I lay back down and buried my face in my damp pillow. I tried to pray, but I felt as if my prayers reached no higher than my ceiling. In the middle of this most horrible night of my life, I heard the lobby buzzer sound to our apartment and then Greg's voice over the intercom. "Lilly? Are you okay? I left you messages. I'm really worried." And then more mumbling that I couldn't hear.

I actually considered running out and letting him in, saying, "Greg! Come up and I'll tell you everything." But I couldn't. I knew he would never be able to handle the entire truth about me. I barely could.

I kept my head under the covers and stayed perfectly still until I heard his car drive away. There is no mistaking the pattering engine of his old VW.

I dried my tears and started hanging up the clothes I couldn't fit in my suitcase. How could this happen? I thought I'd worked all this through. When I'd come to Boston, I'd seen a counselor for a long time. I'd gone to that support group in the church. I thought I was over all of this. Obviously I wasn't. It's easy to get over something when nothing from the old life threatens. But when it does, all of the hard work—all of the working through everything and the long hours of journaling— are for nothing.

I needed to run, but how could I leave all this? Over in the corner was the dresser I'd bought at a garage sale and had stripped and refinished. Next to it, a beautiful antique wooden music stand. Hanging on the wall was a huge paper star light, a gift from Paige's daughter, Sara. On the bed, the handwoven bedspread that I bought at the outdoor market. And on my mirror, photos of me with Greg, and with Bridget.

My thoughts were all over the place on that long and terrible night. *Lord,* I prayed at one point, *let whoever it is lose my e-mail address.* I prayed that the e-mail had been a mistake. I prayed that their hard drive would crash and they'd lose everything. Or they would leave their computer in Starbucks while they went to the restroom, and then when they came back, someone would have run off with it. I was coming up with all sorts of scenarios that God could use. It could happen, couldn't it? God performed all sorts of miracles and I needed a miracle. Now.

At first, I thought the faint knocking was on the door of a neighboring apartment. I ignored it and stayed under my covers. But it persisted. Then I thought I heard someone calling. It wasn't Greg—I had heard him drive away.

More calling. A high-pitched voice. Had Bridget come back without her keys? I roused myself and went toward the door.

More knocking, more calling.

"Yoo-hoo? Bridget? Are you there?" The soft voice sounded like it came from an older woman. Bridget's mother? I put my eye against the peephole. The diminutive, round, ashen-haired woman was not Bridget's mother. The woman outside my door wore an oversized, baggy gray cardigan that I was willing to bet belonged to her husband. Underneath that sweater was a smudgy, food-stained apron tied over crimson track pants. Her sturdy, square hands held out a silver metal cake tin that looked familiar. Curious, I opened the door.

"Yes?"

She looked past me, craned her neck, then looked back at me. "Am I at the wrong apartment?"

"What are you looking for?"

"Bridget." Then she stopped and smiled widely. She was missing several top teeth along the side. "Oh, you must be the roommate."

I was curious about something else. "How did you get in here, may I ask? How did you get in the main door without buzzing?"

"Oh, that," she said, walking around me and into the apartment. "It's the same with my place. People are always leaving the front doors of these places unlocked, or they're propping the doors open. People just don't want to be bothered with keys anymore so they leave a brick in the doorway. Around here it's so safe anyway." She placed the cake tin on the counter like she'd been here before. "You just tell Bridget, dear, that I loved the cookies, and that I do want her recipe."

"Okay, then." I just stood and watched her. She peered up at me with tiny, close-spaced eyes.

"You don't look so well, dear. Is it the flu?"

"No, uh…" I put a hand to my face. Did I look that bad?

She pointed at me. "You know what you need? Some of Bridget's chicken soup. She actually got the recipe from me, you know," she said, aiming a finger at her heart. She shambled through the door, "Now dear, don't forget to tell Bridget that I was here."

I nodded and she was down the steps before I even had a chance to ask who she was. I have to admit that meeting the strange little woman with the square hands and the cake tin had cheered me up for a few minutes.

Bridget came in around ten-thirty. She kicked off her shoes and came over to where I was nestled into a blanket, watching *Law and Order.*

"There's some decaf on," I said.

"Great. Thanks. Oh, these shoes. If I had to wear them one more minute, I swear I would be throwing them against the wall."

"How was the dinner?"

She ran her slender fingers through her hair. "Oh, you know. Company dinners. They go on and on, speech after speech until not only do you want to start throwing shoes, but also pieces of the rubber chicken they serve."

"Now there's a sight I'd like to see."

She went to pour herself a cup of coffee. "Oh, sweet. My recipe exchanger brought my cake tin by."

"Cute little woman," I said. "She told me I needed some of your chicken soup."

"On Saturday, I'll make you some. I surely will. It's good for what ails you."

"How about a broken heart?"

She came back over to me, all concern.

"I've been praying for you all evening. It's what got me through the speeches. And it came to me that this thing with you and Greg, I think it's just a temporary obstacle, like a speed bump in the road." She sat on the couch beside me. "You two belong together. You'll figure it out, Lilly. I just know it. He loves you, you love him."

"I don't know if that's enough now." I shook my head. "I'm this close to a commitment, and I find I just can't do it. I can't explain it."

Bridget took off her suit jacket and pulled her legs up underneath her. "Honey, I know you and Greg belong together. You'll find a way."

I didn't sleep well that night. Sometime in the wee hours of the morning, when it was still dark, I felt hungry. I got up, went into the kitchen nook and poured myself a bowl of Rice Krispies. I stood for a long time at the back window and looked out into the dark yard between the apartments. I could just make out the very old and mostly rusted chain-link fence dividing the so-called backyards. It had a number of ripped-out places, where small animals could easily get through. We'd never gotten around to putting up curtains, but being so far up, we didn't worry too much.

As I gazed into the night sky, the thought came to me that things might be better if I was totally honest with everyone. People only knew half my story. Greg needed to know everything about me, and Bridget needed to know much more than the little bits and pieces I'd chosen to share. Because my story is so much more than living with an abusive boyfriend. My story involves murder, drugs and betrayal—and that's just the beginning.

I looked toward Bridget's door. If she were to come out right now, I'd tell her. I'd make her sit down on the couch and I'd tell her all about Moira and how I'd betrayed the one true friend I'd had in all the world.

And I'd tell Greg, too. I'd call him first thing in the morning and we'd meet for lunch and by the end of it he would know everything as well. And then he would leave me. I knew the particular heartache that Greg carried, and if Greg knew what I had done, what I was, he would run—not walk—away from me.

Greg had been married before. For two years, he

was happily married to his high-school sweetheart. From all accounts, she was a dear, sweet girl—a pastor's daughter. She'd been killed by a young woman who was driving while high on drugs. It had taken a long time for Greg to work through his grief and forgiveness. And I wasn't sure he had, not completely. We'd talked about that. He'd told me how difficult it was for him to find any love in his heart for the person who had killed his wife, and how he carried these feelings of rage over to any drug user who got behind the wheel. I have told him a lot of things, but never that I had regularly used drugs. How could I? How could I tell him that I could have been the young woman who killed his wife?

I was about to pour myself another bowl of cereal when it hit me. If what I was beginning to suspect was true—that Mudd was alive and had tracked me down and sent the e-mail—then no one was safe. Mudd was vicious beyond all viciousness. I put the cereal back without eating any more. Had I actually seen Mudd die? Not really. I'd seen Mark, the owner of the bar holding the gun on Mudd. And that's when I turned and ran. I heard the shot when I got to the van.

I couldn't tell Greg I had been found. That would put him in as much danger as I was in. And I couldn't tell Bridget—dear, sweet, innocent Bridget.

I put away the milk and went back to the rocking chair where I rocked quietly for a while in the dark, thinking, thinking. Because if Mudd had been alive all this time, then my betrayal of Moira was all the more acute.

I went to bed and practiced the sentences I would say to Greg…until I fell asleep.

* * *

In the morning, Greg called me at eight, just like I figured he would.

"You okay? I came by last night but you must've been asleep. I've been thinking about you all night. In the time I've known you, you've never so much as had a cold."

"Greg?" I said. "Can we meet for lunch?"

"Sure, babe, are you up to it?"

I love it when he calls me "babe." I clutched my cell phone and coughed to cover up a sob. "I need to see you, to talk to you," I said. "It's important."

"Lil? You don't sound good. You sure you're okay?"

"Please! Please don't call me 'Lil.' It's a nickname I hate. Please."

There was silence for a moment. "But I always call you 'Lil.'"

"I know. I know. And I hate it."

"Okay, then, uh, I won't call you 'Lil.' Where should we meet, Primo's?"

"No!" I said, maybe a bit too loudly. "Not Primo's. How about—" I cast about for a place "—how about Griffi's Café?"

"Griffi's Café it is then," he said.

Neil, Tiff, Lora and I had a study-group meeting that morning to work on our joint project. We were studying the composer Bela Bartok to show how his early life in Hungary and the music which surrounded him evidenced itself in his compositions. The whole thing seemed a little pointless now. Isn't that what was causing all my problems? The stuff I'd *surrounded* myself with in my youth? Rock music, selling my soul to the devil for a chance to be a rock star. Someone could do a project on me.

I was usually the first to arrive at the table in the student-union building that we'd claimed as our own. While I waited for the others to saunter in late, I would work on music or homework, or check my e-mail. But today the three of them were already there, engaged in a spirited discussion. Tiff, who reminds me of a pixie with her spiky black hair and tiny body, was moving her hands exaggeratedly as she talked. Neil sat next to her, his expressive fingers aligning the edges of his books precisely as he listened.

I shoved in beside Lora. Neil's eyes were bright. "So, you engaged now?"

I groaned. Why couldn't I have kept my effusiveness to myself? "Do I look like I'm engaged?" I waved my empty ring finger in front of their faces.

"What happened?" Tiff asked, concern on her face.

"I was sick last night. We had to cancel." In the future, I vowed, I would be more circumspect with my life. "We're going to reschedule."

Lora raked her dark fingernails through her long, heavy hair. "I personally don't see the big deal with the institution of marriage anyway."

I really didn't feel like getting into this particular discussion with anyone, so I shrugged and opened my notebook.

Neil grinned, ran his hands with their perfectly clean nails down the perfectly aligned edges of his books and said, "Well, if he doesn't want to marry you, you could always marry me."

"Thanks, Neil," I said as Tiff and Lora laughed.

I got to Griffi's at ten to noon and found a booth by the window. I ordered a coffee and waited. The organic coffee and panini shop was getting crowded. Lots of students came here, but it was located among several office buildings, so the place filled up at lunch hour. It was a good thing I'd arrived before the rush.

I used the time before Greg came to read over the lyric sheet, looking for the final, elusive verse of the worship song. I may as well have been trying to read Greek.

Greg arrived on the dot of noon and scooted in across from me. I looked up at him, at the shock of sun-colored hair that fell onto his forehead, at those expressive eyebrows of his. Today he wore a red shirt emblazoned with Creation Music Festival.

I saw the look on his face, the tentativeness in his eyes. His movements were erratic and uncertain. It was as if he didn't know how to be here with me. How could I do this to him? To us? How could I hurt him? Yet what choice did I have?

"Is…" he asked cautiously "…is everything all right with your health? Is that what this is about, Lilly? I was talking with Bridget. Um…" He licked his lips, swallowed.

My health. That would be the easy way out. I could tell him I was dying and that I had to say goodbye and go live with my parents. And then I could pack my suitcases and disappear. For a quick second, I thought about that. But it wouldn't work. Bridget already knew I wasn't really sick.

More than anything, I wanted to reach across and touch his cheek, tell him how much I loved him. At that precise moment, our perky, smiley waitress came and poured us coffee, chattering happily about the daily specials. We ordered. And then Greg and I were left alone again. I looked down at my coffee cup and couldn't think of what to say.

"Lilly?" He looked at me.

I was shredding the paper napkin in my lap. I said, "I'm not sick. I lied to you about that. I'm just so unsure of things, Greg. I mean about us. I'm just—I don't know where to begin. I had a pretty rough life before I came to Boston. There are so many things I hid from you, so many things about my past. I'm just thinking that, maybe, I don't know…" I ran my finger down the length of my spoon. Then I placed it beside my coffee. At a big square table beside us, a business meeting was forming. I heard cheerful hellos, saw hearty handshakes. People in suits. People with computers. People drinking coffee. I looked at the short, stocky man who seemed to be leading it. He reminded me of an actor whose name I couldn't place.

"I know there's more to your story, Lilly. And I wait and wait for you to feel comfortable enough to share it with me, but that time never comes. I know you're dealing with a lot of issues, but are these issues insurmountable?"

"I don't know, Greg." *They're bigger than you could ever imagine,* I thought, looking past him. "With what I've been through, it's going to take time."

Our bouncy waitress plunked sandwiches down in front of us. I looked at my chicken panini. The sight of it made me feel slightly nauseated. She left after assuring us that she'd be back, and saying if there was anything we wanted, just give her a holler. *How about a new life?* I thought.

"I was just wondering," I said, playing with my spoon again, "if we could just be friends for a while."

"Friends?" Greg pushed his own plate away, reached forward, put my spoon on the table and took my hand. "Lilly, what are you saying?"

"I guess—" I swallowed "—I don't want to break up. That's not what I'm saying."

"But you want us to be just friends," he said.

I nodded. I kept my gaze on my chicken sandwich, memorizing the way it looked on the plate, with the edges curled. It didn't look like food to me.

"There's so much about me you don't know," I said.

"I know." He kept his gaze steady. "Lilly, we've shared a lot with each other these past few months. I know all about the relationship you were in with an incredibly abusive boyfriend, and then how you escaped, how you managed to find your way up here, how you came to faith and how faith in God changed you. I know you've come from a hard place. I probably know more about you than you do, in some ways."

I doubted that, but I let it slide.

"And whatever it is," he continued, "you can trust me. You need to trust me. I love you. I've never met anyone like you before."

I looked across the table and saw the pain in his

eyes. I looked down into my coffee. The silence between us lengthened. Someone at the meeting table laughed out loud. I still didn't say anything.

"So," he said. "Are you going to tell me or not?"

I shook my head. How do I tell him that knowing more about me could put him in danger?

"I can't," I said. "I thought I could but I can't. I'm not ready. Could we just—um, be friends?"

Now it was his turn to shake his head. "I don't think so," he said. "I really don't think so."

We ate the rest of the meal in silence.

I didn't want it to be like this. I wanted us to be engaged and meeting for lunch to plan our spring wedding. I'd told him a lot, yes, but never once had I mentioned the name Mudd to him. Nor had I told him anything about Moira.

FOUR

Days went by. First one. Then the next. When after the third day, I hadn't received a follow-up e-mail, I dared myself to believe that God had answered my prayer. Maybe whoever sent the e-mail did get their laptop stolen at Starbucks. Maybe their hard drive crashed. And maybe, just maybe, Mudd was really dead, like I'd always believed. And then I had another thought. Could the e-mail have come from Moira herself? Was Moira simply wanting to reconnect?

Maybe there had been an accompanying cheery e-mail and Moira, who was never very computer savvy, had lost it, or it just hadn't come through. I was working up all sorts of scenarios in my mind, but the fact was, after four days with no follow up, I was beginning to allow myself to relax. Just a bit. Maybe.

"I think I'm ready to commit to Greg," I told Bridget on the evening of the fifth day. "I think I'm ready to say yes now."

"Well, it's about time, hon! I think that's great."

I put two individual pizzas into the microwave,

plugged in the kettle and cut up an apple. "You want a pizza? I've got two here."

Bridget looked up from her knitting. "Lilly, you should eat better. I could make you something nutritious."

"Chicken soup?"

"Don't knock it."

I grinned at her. "Oh, Bridget, you are such a mother."

"Well, I worry about you is all." She went back to her knitting.

I stood at the window and looked down into the darkened backyards and said, "I don't think I'm afraid anymore. It was just all the stuff from before I came here. When I thought of commitment, it all started coming down on me like a landslide. Plus, I had this scare. I thought someone from my former life was trying to contact me."

"What happened?" She talked without missing a stitch. "You thought you saw someone?"

I shook my head. "I didn't see anyone. I got a weird e-mail. But it was nothing."

As I looked out the window, I noticed that someone had been gardening at the ground-level apartment directly behind ours. The flowers that had been there all summer had been dug up and laid to the side. I knew that whoever lived there was a fastidious gardener. I often looked down at the flowers neatly arranged around the small bricked-in area. Perhaps they were putting in a new deck.

The microwave dinged. Despite the fact that Bridget

didn't think microwave pizza was very nutritious, I put one on a plate for her. She ate it quite happily while we watched the news.

On the morning of the sixth day with no more strange e-mails, I decided to let Greg back in. I came up with a plan. I called Neil for help.

"Can you do this for me?"

"For you, Lilly, of course. I may even get Tiff to help. She'd be good at that."

I said, "I've got all the songs on my flash drive. I can drive that over to you."

"No need," he said. "They're on my hard drive."

I phoned Primo's and made reservations for Greg and me for the following evening. I told them it was special.

"We were so sorry when you had to cancel last week." I recognized Maria's voice. She and her husband, Peter, ran Primo's.

"Consider this the official reschedule," I said.

"But," she paused, "I don't know." She seemed hesitant and I couldn't for the life of me figure out why—unless they were booked solid, but that seemed unlikely. She went on, "This was going to be a surprise for you, no?"

Ah, so my theory was right. Greg had been planning on proposing. "Not anymore. Now the very same surprise is for *him*."

That was my second mistake. My first was thinking that nothing had changed since last week.

I went to the church with coffees for everyone. I was nervous. I hadn't seen Greg since Griffi's. I'd walked out ahead of him and when I'd turned to say goodbye, he was gone.

I had to walk through yet another detour, down another dingy hallway, and through the basement which was, I saw, piled high with all kinds of workmen's tools and boards and Sheetrock. And then it was back up the stairs and into the office, but at least I knew my way now. Several workmen greeted me with hellos as I went past.

When I finally got to Greg's office, after dropping off coffees for Brenda and Dave, I saw that it was even in more disarray than a week ago. The wall that used to contain his bookshelves had been entirely removed, and through the gaping hole, I could see a couple of guys hammering. Despite the fact that we were on display, I put the coffees on the desk, kissed him quickly on the cheek and said, "Keep tomorrow open."

"Tomorrow?" he said.

I playfully put my fingers to my lips and said, "Shh, it's a surprise."

Here was my plan: I was going to let Greg propose to me. I had a feeling he would bring the ring. And if he didn't get around to proposing to me? I'd propose to him. I'm a perfectly modern woman and pefectly modern women are well within their rights to make the marriage proposal these days. I could picture us twenty-five years from now, Greg telling people, "And when she asked me to marry her? How could I say no?" And then I'd laugh and say, "I only asked him because I knew he was going to ask me the week before."

"Any hints as to where we're going?" he asked, looking doubtful.

I grinned and batted my eyelashes theatrically at him. "It's a total, one-hundred-percent surprise."

Greg frowned slightly, and rubbed his cheek where I'd kissed him. "Lilly?" The expression on his face was part hurt, part confusion and part hope. "What's this all about?"

I grinned. "Can't I come up with a surprise for you? A secret?"

"Your eyes," he said.

"What?" I put my hand to my face, wondering if my mascara was running.

"You don't seem like yourself." He frowned and looked over to where two workmen were mixing paint and chatting. They couldn't hear us.

"What about my eyes?"

"Right now—I don't know—your eyes seem too bright or something."

"Too bright?" This wasn't going entirely as planned. Why wasn't he more enthusiastic? Maybe because the last time we'd seen each other we had a fight? "Okay, here's the deal, Greg. Just erase this past week. It never existed. Rewind the video. Tomorrow night, everything will be changed. You'll see. I'll pick you up at six-thirty. Be ready, okay?"

"It's really not so easy to erase an entire week from a person's mind."

"I made a mistake, Greg. I was scared. I shouldn't have cancelled our original night out. But now I want to make amends. I have seen the error of my ways…" I batted my eyelashes at him again. And then I quickly stopped, remembering what he'd just said about my eyes. "Greg, what I'm trying to say is this. I want to make it up to you. I've changed my mind about our relationship. I want to pick up where we left off a week ago."

"If you say so."

Greg said nothing.

"Well then, I'll see you," I said. I was standing close enough for him to kiss me. If he wanted to.

He reached down and picked up a piece of paper from his desk and studied it. "Yeah," he said, without looking at me.

My next stop was the college cafeteria where I was meeting Neil. I couldn't dwell on Greg's less than enthusiastic response. It would all be fixed soon. Tomorrow night, we would be engaged and then this whole dreadful week would be history.

I should have realized, however, that Greg's lack of enthusiasm was merely a shadow of things to come.

My equivalent of an engagement ring for him was going to be a CD of my own compositions. Over the past six months, I'd written three love songs for Greg, songs he'd never heard; I'd been saving them for the precisely right moment. And this was it. I had recorded them with the help of Neil and Tiff and converted them to MP3s on my computer. When I'd recorded the first one, Neil's eyes had widened behind his thick glasses and his mouth formed itself into an O making him look like an owl.

"That one—" he'd raised his hands excitedly "—that one would be good with some cello behind it."

"Yeah," Tiff had said. "As subtle undertones, like a drone, almost."

Neil was a perfectionist and an expert at mastering. When I asked him yesterday if there was any way he could possibly find the time to take these three songs, remaster them, maybe add some strings, cello or piano perhaps, he said, "No problem." It would be an honor, he told me. And he was sure that Tiff could help. Tiff has a good ear, he added. I agreed.

I was sitting in the cafeteria, waiting for him to show up with my brand-new engagement CD and planning my night—what to wear, what to say, how to act, how to do my hair, how to erase the past week from the universe. I was browsing through a wedding planning Web site when I looked up.

Neil stood there, his hair perfectly combed, wearing a brown jacket that looked like it belonged to someone's father. He was holding out the CD and smiling broadly.

"Hey, hello," I said, closing the lid of my computer.

He placed the CD down on the table in front of me. "I was up until two in the morning," he said, "but I got it done. And I think you're going to like it. I even recorded a bit of me on cello. Tiff had some good suggestions. We both worked on it."

I picked it up. I was on the cover, sitting on a piano stool and holding my guitar. "Where'd the picture come from?" I asked.

"It was on your church Web site."

"Really?" I hadn't realized there were so many pictures of me on the Web site. I felt a fuzzy unease, a touch of chill in my spine, but quickly dismissed it. The e-mail meant nothing. It was a week ago. Everything was fine now.

I opened the case and examined the CD. He'd printed a label for it with "All My Love" and a place for me to sign. "This is cool, Neil. You are such a great person to do this for me."

"We want you to be happy."

There were even liner notes. I pulled them out and flattened them on the table. He'd spent a lot of time on this. He pointed at the words of the three songs surrounded by flowers and hearts. "That was Tiff's idea. She did the artwork. She's good at that."

I turned the notes over. "It's beautiful. You guys did a great job. Thank you!"

"I knew you wanted it to be special."

I looked up at him, at the innocent earnestness in those brown eyes. "You're a romantic, Neil," I said. Neil wasn't every girl's cup of tea. He was a little too studious looking, his hair was usually a bit too precisely combed and he wasn't much of a dresser. "What you need," I found myself saying, "is a nice young woman of your own who you can regale with flowers and music on a regular basis."

"I do have a nice young woman that I'm in love with, but she doesn't know I exist, at least not in that way," he said.

Tiff, I bet it's Tiff, I thought, as she waved at us from across the cafeteria. His eyes brightened as he said goodbye and took off toward her. They left the cafeteria together.

It started to rain and big dollops hit the large plate-glass windows. I watched some students scurrying for cover. Others were oblivious, it seemed. I saw Tiff and Neil scamper into the nearest building.

In my mind, I went back to a place where a lost girl sat in the backseat of a Greyhound bus in the middle of a downpour. She held a dirty backpack tightly.

She ignored the people coming and going to the cubicle washroom behind her: mothers with small children, old people, teens. And when anyone tried to make casual conversation with her, she turned her face away toward the rain-smeared windows, the backpack clutched even more fiercely to her.

She was heading north. She didn't know where. But the one thing she did know was that she could never go back. Not now. Not ever. She realized this while streaks of rain ran like rivers on the window beside her…

I opened up my computer again. I don't know why, but I clicked on the picture of the girl. I guess I needed to see her one more time before I deleted her. She was singing. I knew the song, I knew every song she sang, because I'd written all of them.

FIVE

I'm a jeans and boots and sweater sort of person. For my big date with Greg, I decided to wear a brand-new pair of jeans with my nicest black boots. Instead of my usual sweater, I chose a long-sleeved, black cashmere top with glittery bits scattered across the front. My mother had given it to me for Christmas. It was beautiful, but I seldom wore it—it was too sparkly for church, and I would never wear something so New Year's Eve-y to school or work. But it seemed just about perfect for tonight. And it would look quite nice set off with a glinting diamond ring on my left hand.

Bridget wasn't home and wouldn't be until later, so she didn't get to listen to the CD with me. I was impressed with what Neil had done. He'd made my three songs sound beautiful—and professional—with the perfect arrangement of strings, cello and percussion.

It was cool and windy as I drove through the Boston traffic to Greg's apartment. The CD was wrapped up with a big red bow and tucked in my bag. As soon as Greg asked me to marry him—as I was sure he would—

as soon as he brought out the ring—as I was sure he would—I would put up my hand as if to say "wait," whereupon I would reach into my bag, grab the CD and while I said a huge "yes," I would lay it down in front of him. It would be one of those romantic and touching moments, and I planned to try very hard to record it in my head, so when I got home, I could write it all down.

And if perchance he didn't ask me, I would ask him.

It didn't work out that way.

As I drove to Greg's house, it occurred to me again that maybe I should tell him my entire story—Moira, the money I took and the murder. Maybe I should be completely honest with the man I intended to spend the rest of my life with. Or maybe not. Maybe I'd tell him after we married. But that didn't seem right either.

I saw Greg before he saw me. He was standing in front of his house leaning against a lamppost, hands stuffed into his pockets. He wore khakis, a blue windbreaker and a pensive look on his face, something I could see even from this distance. He seemed nervous as he stood there, eyes darting this way and that. He hadn't seen me yet.

I slowed in front of him, and he gave me an uncertain smile. I'd seen that smile before, when he was unsure about something or had heard a joke that he didn't think was funny. I stopped the car and he slid into the passenger seat, bringing the cold in with him.

"Hi," he said.

I greeted him with a wide smile and pulled away from the curb. "Hey," he said. His voice was quiet, gentle. I looked briefly at his amazing blue eyes, at the crinkles around them. He saw me looking at him and quickly moved his gaze away from me. Why wouldn't he look at me?

"Greg?" I said.

"Yeah?" he answered, looking out the window.

"You want to know where we're going?" I grinned mischievously at him.

Silence. A moment passed.

He shrugged. "If you want to tell me."

"So, you want it to be a surprise, then?" I asked.

"Whatever you want."

"How come you're not being more cooperative?" I said, trying to tease him. I glanced over and he still wasn't smiling.

"Cooperative about what?"

"You're just not your usual self." And he wasn't. He was usually so chatty that I never had to carry the conversation.

I thought he said, "Maybe I'm a bit confused," but I couldn't be sure, he spoke so quietly.

"What?"

"I said, 'Maybe I'm a bit tired.'"

I nodded. More silence. Maybe the renovation of his office was getting to him. And having to reorganize everything. That would do it to anyone, wouldn't it? That's what it was. And as soon as that was all over with, things would all be right again.

And we'd be engaged.

We were in Primo's parking lot before I knew it, and I pulled into a space right in front.

"Oh, wow," I said, forcing myself to be cheerful. "Look, a perfect parking spot. That must be a good omen."

"Primo's," he said. "We were going to come here last week."

"Yep, Primo's," I said with as much enthusiasm as I could muster. "We're a week late, but I don't think they'll mind!"

Greg said nothing as he got out of the car.

We didn't hold hands when we walked together into the restaurant. Things were not going as planned, and I didn't quite know why.

The staff at Primo's was awaiting our arrival. The owner's daughter Lucia, who worked as a waitress, greeted us. In a floor-length dress of lavender satin, with her dark hair piled on top of her head in an array of big brown curls, I wondered if she was on her way to the prom. I was about to ask her when I realized that all the waiters, waitresses and kitchen staff were formally clad. The guys wore tuxes and the girls were in gowns. And they were grinning at us.

I couldn't help myself. I grabbed his arm and said, "Greg! Is this what you planned for last week?"

He stood for several seconds and ran his hand over his face. He looked like he would rather be anywhere but at Primo's. I tried again, "This is so nice, Greg! You are so romantic! I had no idea."

Lucia led us to the table in the corner by the window. It was not our regular Primo's table with gouges in the wood and a flimsy metal napkin dispenser. It had been covered with a dazzling white tablecloth and a tall white candle sat in the center. I kept watching Greg's face. Why wasn't he smiling?

He took off his jacket and placed it on the back of

his chair. Underneath, he wore a crisp blue shirt which made his eyes even bluer than usual. Someone had moved a couple of floor plants close to the table, giving us more privacy. Lucia sat us down and, with great flourish, unfolded cloth napkins, placing them in our laps.

"Lucia," I said, finally finding my voice. "You look so pretty. Everyone does."

"This is my prom dress. My mom suggested it. She said you guys were having a special night—that's why we're all dressed up. We did this last week, too, but you had to cancel. So I had to waitress all night in my prom dress!"

I gave her an awkward smile.

From behind the counter the staff eyed us. Peter kept looking at us, grinning and then running back into the kitchen.

I told Lucia what a nice touch the candle was and was suddenly aware that I was doing all the talking. Greg had said not a word since we'd arrived. *Not one.* I picked up the menu and pretended to study it, but kept casting glances at Greg. He was frowning down at his menu, which was flat on the table.

Lucia filled our water glasses.

"Isn't this nice?" I said to Greg after she'd gone. "And I know you planned all this. I know you did." I added a bit of a giggle at the end of my sentence. But it felt fake and simpering and I was beginning to realize that something was not just a little wrong, but seriously wrong.

He nodded. "It *is* nice." His voice was flat.

At that moment, Lucia was standing beside us again. "And what would signor and signorina wish for tonight? The usual?"

When Greg didn't respond, I said, "Yes, the usual."

The usual was two Cokes and a supreme pizza with the works. We always got a large. They divided up the leftovers into two containers which we took to our respective homes for later. Greg said he always ate his cold the next day for breakfast. I always took mine to college and heated it for lunch in the microwave.

She gathered up the menus and left.

More silence.

"Greg," I said, "are you okay?"

"Fine." His hands were in his lap. I hoped that he was nervous and quiet because he was getting the ring box out of his pocket. He brought his hands back up to the table. No ring box.

More awkward silence.

"Um, Greg?"

"Yeah?" He looked at me.

"Tell me about that youth conference you're going to."

He shrugged. "Not much to tell."

Greg could usually be counted on to go on about the worship band alone for twenty minutes. I knew something was terribly wrong, but I didn't know how to fix it.

"You sure everything's okay?"

"Why shouldn't it be?"

"I don't know," I said.

"You don't know what?" he asked.

"Why it shouldn't be okay," I responded.

I tried to make my eyes sparkle, I was trying to smile coyly and sweetly, but I didn't think I was managing it. And I didn't think it would help at this point anyway. I was beginning to feel that I would rather be anywhere but here.

"The plants are a nice touch. Did you arrange all this?" I asked.

He sighed. It was audible. "I did. But that was a week ago." Signifying, of course, that a lot can happen in a week.

"I know. I'm glad we were able to reschedule. Why don't we make this week last week?"

"I already told you, Lilly. It's not easy to erase an entire week out of your life," was what he said.

"You remember what I told you in Griffi's, about us only being friends? Well, I've changed my mind about that. I'm ready to, um, to not be just friends anymore."

He stared into my eyes without saying anything. Then he looked at the candle, which flickered, then at me again.

"Well, at least the pizza should be good," he mumbled.

I excused myself and walked with shaky legs to the ladies' room, where I looked at myself in the mirror. My face was too pale. My hair, which I had taken great pains with, had all frizzed out at the sides. I added some blush, patted my hair down, put on more lipstick. My fingers shook as I applied mascara. A clump of black landed under my right eye. I stopped, forcing myself to breathe deeply. I felt at any moment I was going to burst into tears. I ran a piece of Kleenex in the tap and dabbed it under my eye. I worked and worked until I looked passable. But as I left the ladies' room I realized that no amount of makeup would cover up the past week, or my past life.

By the time I was back at our table, which suddenly looked gaudy, embarrassing and out of place, Lucia had put plates at our respective places.

I prayed that our pizza would come soon, and this night would be over with. I told Greg how nice his shirt looked. I asked if it was new and he said it was. All small talk now. Two strangers.

Our pizza arrived; Lucia set it on a metal rack with a flame underneath. Without a word, Greg put a slice on my plate. We chewed our pizza in the quiet and sipped our Cokes in silence. The gallantly clad kitchen staff kept looking out at us—even they seemed to sense that something was wrong. A few more moments of silence and I wanted the floor to open up and swallow me. I decided to try one more time.

"Greg?"

"Hmm?"

"What's going on? Will you please tell me?"

"Last week you had your week of confusion. Now it's my turn."

I looked down at my pizza, suddenly nauseous. "Okay, I can accept that." Except this was a Greg I didn't know. In the six months I'd known him, I'd only seen the jovial, easygoing, chatty Greg, not the sullen, confused one.

He gave himself a second piece and tried to talk

about the youth conference. But it sounded like he was reciting facts, filling in the blank conversation spaces with meaningless words. I kept saying "wow" and "that sounds good," but it was a conversation I could very well be having with someone I didn't know who happened to be giving me the rundown on the conference. A telemarketer. A salesperson.

By the time our spumoni came, I was completely lost, with no idea what to do or say. By the time we got in the car, I felt an incredible sadness. When I dropped him off, he gave me a peck on the cheek and quickly got out of the car.

I cried all the way home.

SIX

"Well?" Bridget met me at the door. "Are you now the proud owner of a diamond ring? Let's see, let's see!"

I waved my ringless hand in the air without saying anything. Her face fell.

"It didn't go well. Have some pizza," I said and put the white Primo's box on our coffee table.

She stared at me. "How can I possibly eat pizza when you just told me that it didn't go well? Lilly, you look like you've been crying."

I sat down heavily on the couch and sighed deeply. A couple of deep breaths might just keep me from blubbering all over the place. Bridget was standing in front of me, looking fabulous in a pair of gray sweats with a tiny hole in the knee and a T-shirt. Which, by the way, made me feel worse because she always looks so great and I can never quite manage it. And then I felt even worse for having those thoughts.

"And what do you mean it didn't go well?" she asked.

"I mean he didn't ask me to marry him."

"But then you asked him, right? What about the CD?"

I patted my bag. "Still in here. Safe and sound."

"But what happened?"

"Nothing, actually. Greg was like this completely different person. He barely said two words the entire time. No, correct that—once he got talking about a conference he's going to, he talked and talked. But it was never personal. The subject of marriage never came up. And of course, I humiliated myself by saying that I was ready to commit. After which he said nothing, after which I went to the ladies' room. That's about it." I felt old and tired as I huddled into the corner of the couch and pulled the comforter more firmly up to my neck.

She touched my shoulder, and the tears started again, slightly at first, and then I sobbed while she hugged me. When I finally regained my composure, I said, "I've made such a mess of things. I never should've canceled last week. Now he's changed his mind."

"No, he hasn't. He's just confused about last week. You two belong together, Lilly. It'll work out."

I found a balled up tissue in my pocket and blew my nose. She went and got the Kleenex box from the kitchen table and placed it down between us. I took three more. She said, "I'm so sorry, Lilly. This must be awful for you. Is there anything I can get you? Some tea?"

"Maybe some tea would be nice."

"I'll get tea." She got up and plugged in the kettle, then came back and sat beside me. I told her about how the staff was all dressed up and that the table had a candle, and that this was what Greg had planned for the week before, and how I didn't even take the CD out of my bag, and how my whole plan to ask him to marry me backfired.

When the kettle whistled, she went to the kitchen and made tea while I went on about my horrible night. "I never should've cancelled last week. That was the biggest mistake of my life."

She stood curiously on one leg and bit into a piece of the leftover pizza. Then she asked, "Why *did* you cancel? I've never quite understood that. Not entirely."

I took a breath. "Remember that e-mail I told you about? The one I said was nothing?"

"You thought someone from the past was contacting you, right?"

"Yeah, I thought it was from Mudd."

"Mudd?" She leaned against the window, looking at me. I had told her about my relationship with Mudd, but I had never told her his name before.

"That was his name. That's what we all called him. And last week, I thought I got an e-mail from him. Which is impossible, because he's dead. But when I got this e-mail, I was convinced he was back and stalking me. But now I know it must've been someone else."

"Was it a threatening e-mail?"

"I think so. It scared me at first, and brought everything back. I was in such a horrible place back then, and I did some really awful things. I was no angel. That's why I was so worried when I got that e-mail, and why

I was so unsure about marrying Greg. Because of the threat of my old life."

"Did you answer the e-mail?"

I shook my head, wondering if I should have answered it. Had it come from Moira? What if she was trying to reconnect?

"But now you think the e-mail was just some sort of fluke? Like spam?"

"I don't know," I said. "I just don't know."

She put both feet flat on the floor and held the pizza in her hand. "I know you've worked hard to get to a new place. You're a new creature in Christ now—everything is different. You're an amazing person, Lilly. You don't have to go back to that place, even in your mind. Did you tell Greg about the e-mail?"

"No." I glanced over at the kitchen window, looking through it to the black sky.

She said very quietly, "Is Mudd the guy who died that morning when you were at the bar?"

I nodded. I'd told Bridget about that morning, how Mudd had dragged me out of bed and taken me to the bar where I'd seen Mark, the owner, pick up the gun and aim it at Mudd. I'd been running for the van when I heard the gunshot.

"What I've never understood in all of this is why you never went to the police."

"That thought never entered my head then. I was young and stupid and on drugs most of the time. The police wouldn't have believed me. At least that's what I thought then."

"Does Greg know any of this?"

"Bits and pieces," I said.

"Maybe," she said, "maybe you should tell him your whole story."

"If I did, he would have nothing more to do with me. Because of his first wife."

She started. "What do you mean? The fact that he was married before has nothing to do with you. You feel you can't compare with her? You're the only woman he's allowed himself to care about since she died, he'd told me once how he thought he could never love anyone again—how he felt he would never forgive the girl who drove the car that night—and then you came along."

"That's just it," I whispered. "I could have been that girl."

She shook her head vigorously. "No, Lilly, don't even say things like that. What you need to do is to fight for Greg. Do whatever you can to get him back. Your old life is over. You should never forget that."

I was lost in thought for several minutes, pondering Bridget's words, while she stood at the window, her hand on her hip.

"I'm worried about Mrs. Eberline," she said, suddenly. Bridget has a habit of changing the subject of conversations quite abruptly. I know that in her mind, one thought quite naturally segues into the next, but for the person on the other end of the conversation, the effect can be quite jarring. I stared at her for a moment, trying to comprehend what she was talking about.

"Who's Mrs. Eberline?" I finally managed.

She sighed. "Lilly, you *met* her. She was the one who returned the cake tin."

"Why are you worried about her?"

"Well, her backyard for one," said Bridget.

"What do you mean 'her backyard'?"

Bridget pointed through the kitchen window. "All that dirt and deck that's been torn up. She would've told me if she were doing any renovations. I mean, the woman talks about everything, so it's surprising she didn't mention that."

I got off the couch and joined Bridget at the window. "You mean that's where she lives? I thought she was someone from church."

"No, she lives back there, and she loves her flowers. She puts all the rest of us to shame. Even Gert from next door says so."

I stared at her, smiling. "Bridget, how do you *know* all this?"

She turned and faced me. "I grew up in the country, where we make it a point to know our neighbors. I guess it's so ingrained in me that I've brought that attitude with me to the city."

"And you know who lives below us and beside us?" I had not a clue.

Her eyes went wide. "Of course, Lilly! This is our building! We have to know our neighbors. Everyone should know their neighbors."

I shook my head, amazed, but she was already looking back out the window. "It just seems so odd that she would do all this in the fall. The ground is going to freeze soon."

She handed me a cup of tea and we sat for a while, trying to chat about other things including Mrs. Eberline, but my thoughts kept scrambling back to Greg.

* * *

Later in my room, I sat cross-legged on my bed, propped a couple of pillows behind my back and positioned my laptop on my knees. It was finally time to erase that picture from my computer. I would look one last time into the eyes of that sad, bruised girl with the voice that drew people to her despite themselves. I would look at her and then I would put her photograph in the trash, then erase the trash. And then it would be over. And I would fight to get Greg back.

While I looked at her and remembered, I prayed and thanked God that my life was different now, that he had answered my prayers, and that I'd had no more e-mails to contend with. I placed my finger on the girl's face, said goodbye and then dragged the e-mail with its attachment to my trash.

Feeling relieved, I clicked on Inbox. I stared at a new e-mail that had just come in. The subject line read, "PAY ATTENTION THIS TIME, LCJ." I gasped when I saw it. It was the same girl in a different pose. She was not alone in this picture, behind her on the stage were two female backup singers, a drummer, a lead guitarist and a bass player. But the painfully thin girl with the blue-black hair was out front. Her guitar hung by its strap on her bony body, but she wasn't playing it. In one hand she held the microphone and with the other she pointed fiercely at the audience, her long hair falling forward in strings across her angry face.

I couldn't move.

The whole thing wasn't over. It wasn't over by a long shot. I hugged my pillow. I rocked back and forth on my bed and groaned. My carefully constructed house of cards was falling down around me, one card at a time. While I stared at the black-haired girl, more e-mails began arriving in my in-box, many, many of them, too many of them.

Quickly they filled up my entire screen. They were all addressed to LCJ, and they all came from the same Hotmail account. They continued to download, screen after screen. I put my computer on my dresser and faced it away from me. I went into the bathroom and tried to get ready for bed. When I came back, they were still coming through. I turned off my light.

But of course I couldn't sleep. Sometime in the early hours of the morning, I reached for my laptop—the screen was now black. When I pressed the space bar, it jiggled to life and I brought it onto my bed with me. A little box with red letters flashed at me, saying I'd exceeded my mailbox quota. I was reminded that if I cleared my trash, I could again send and receive messages. I clicked OK. Five hundred and thirteen messages had managed to download before my mailbox had filled. All had attached pictures of the same black-haired girl. Different poses, but the same girl. I was going to trash them all but decided against it. It came to me that, if I was going to fight this like Bridget suggested, if I ever went to the police about this, I might need these pictures. I began the laborious process of transferring them into my picture folder.

There were photos of the girl on stage playing her guitar, candid shots of her with friends, staged shots of her in black leather, posters announcing upcoming concerts and some images I didn't want to look at, including pictures of the girl in suggestive poses. There were so many of these that I was disgusted. I didn't want to save these particular photos, but knew I had to.

There was one picture, however, that made my blood turn cold. It was the very last that came through and I choked when I saw it. It was a photo of an army-surplus backpack. It wasn't, of course, the specific backpack that I'd stolen from Mudd. A very long time ago, I'd stuffed that particular backpack deep within a Dumpster behind McDonald's, five states away from here. But it was similar, similar enough that I knew it was a warning. *Remember this? I do. You messed with me. I have found you. Now I'm coming for you.*

SEVEN

In the morning I called our Internet provider and canceled our account. Was I unhappy with the service? No, I said. Did I want to try the ultrahigh speed for three weeks at the same price as high speed? No, I didn't want anything for now. The truth was, I planned to go with a different internet provider altogether for a clean start. What I needed was a new e-mail. This wasn't something I needed to run by Bridget. Her e-mail address came from work and would remain the same. My e-mail address would change, however, and that's exactly what I wanted.

I came out to the kitchen and told Bridget what I'd done.

"You did that this morning already?" She was standing tall in black heels and a burgundy suit, pouring skim milk onto a small bowl of granola.

I told her that I had received another e-mail. I kept it singular. I didn't tell her that five hundred and thirteen e-mails had made their way into my computer. I said I needed a new e-mail address and that's why I'd changed our service provider.

"Lilly!" she said, her eyes wide. "What does this mean?"

"What this means is that Mudd is alive. That's what this means."

"Then you need to go to the police! Now you really do. Can I see the e-mail?"

"I've deleted it," I lied. How could I let Bridget see that girl? I went on, "Last night you said I should fight. Well, getting a new e-mail account is the first step."

"Well, good then. And going to the police is the second step." It wasn't a question. It was a statement.

"I will, I promise," I lied. Again.

Bridget gave me a big hug. "Lilly, I just want you to know that I'll be praying for you all day."

"Thanks, Bridget."

After she left I pulled on my good blue pants and a sweater while I stood at my bedroom window and looked over at the church. Cars and vans with construction logos along the sides were already parked out front.

I pulled on my jacket and headed out into the morning. There was a chill in the air which exactly matched the chill in my mood. As I walked toward the church, I kept catching myself with a sob in the back of my throat. It was probably for the best, our not getting engaged last night. Because now I knew that Mudd was alive. There are certain things about my old life that I *couldn't* let Greg know.

The sob I felt in my throat was such a physical thing that it surprised me: I hurt right down to the bottom of my toes and nothing seemed real.

I walked rapidly past the church.

There were cheese danishes in the staff room at the music store. It occurred to me that I hadn't had breakfast, yet I couldn't eat, wasn't hungry. I wondered if I would ever be able to eat again. Rob, my boss, grinned as he bounced toward me on tip toes. When he walks, he prances on the balls of his feet with his trousers belted high. He's an expert guitar technician as well as a true eccentric.

"How are you, Lilly?" he asked.

"I'm okay," I said, hanging up my jacket. Even though Rob is a sweetie, I really didn't want to get into this with him.

Midway through the busy morning, when it was quiet, I decided to make a long-overdue phone call. There are so many times I wish I had a mother I could go to when things got tough, a mother who would take me shopping and then to Friendly's so we could drown our sorrows in strawberry milk shakes. I sat on the edge of the piano bench in the practice room and pressed my mom's cell number into my phone.

"Hello?" I heard my mother's tight voice. She sounded in a hurry, but she always sounds in a hurry, basically because she always is. I gripped my phone more tightly.

When I was a little girl, my mother didn't have a lot of time for me. I don't remember ever sitting in her lap and feeling her smooth my hair, telling me everything will be okay. On the other hand, she was always full of practical advice. She works in a bank and gives financial advice to the very wealthy. If I ever won the lottery, she'd be the one I'd go to. But for broken hearts, she doesn't have a clue. Yet, for some reason, I still wanted to try.

It was my father who came to my piano recitals when I was a kid and encouraged me to study voice. It was my father who persuaded my mother that they needed to provide for whatever the music scholarship didn't cover. She was only convinced when my father used phrases like "a sensible expenditure" and "good return on investment."

There's a part of me that thinks I walked away from their money and the scholarship because of my mother's indifference. I wanted her to see me as a real person rather than an investment. I don't think she ever has.

"Mom?" I said.

"Lil? Is that you, Lil?"

"Hi, Mom." I thought I could hear the jingle of a ring of keys. I could picture her: suited, hair neatly coifed, her keys in one hand, the phone in the other. "Are you on your way out?" I asked.

"Actually, yes, Lil, but it's nice to hear your voice. Even though I've got to run."

"I thought I was phoning on your cell phone."

"Nope, kiddo, this is the home number."

"Mom?"

"Yes?"

"Mom? Um—"

"Lil? I don't mean to interrupt, but before I forget, did that man ever reach you?"

I sat still on the piano bench, my knees pressed together. "What are you talking about?" Through the plate-glass window of the practice room, I could see Rob and a customer bent over an electronic piano.

"Some man called, looking for you. About a month ago now, maybe longer. That's how long it's been since we've talked. He wanted your e-mail."

A man called? I stood up, put a hand to my forehead. "Mom? This is important. Who was he? Did you give him my e-mail? What did he sound like?"

"Is this some guy from one of those Internet dating services? I hope you're not wasting your time on those things. So many of them are run by scam artists—"

"Mom!"

"What?" She seemed startled by my tone.

"This is really important. Who was this man? Did you give him my e-mail?"

"Of course not. I would never do that and neither would your father. He was the one who took the call."

"Did the man give his name?" My head was spinning. "Can I talk to Dad?"

"No, Lil. He's at the university already."

I could have guessed that. My father is a chemistry professor who spent most mornings in his office. "So you don't know who he was or anything?"

"Nope, but you could call your father and ask."

"I will."

We chatted a few more minutes, while my thoughts continued to swirl. I never got around to telling her about my particular heartbreak, not that she'd had time anyway. When we said goodbye, I called my father's extension at the university and left a message on his voice-mail.

The phone call had me so unnerved it took several minutes before I could go back out into the store. A man had called? But how would this man, whoever he was, know my parents' phone number? I had never told Mudd anything about my parents. Moira had no idea where my parents lived, or even their names. In our group back then, we didn't talk about family. They didn't exist in our world. I had met Mudd's mother and brother but they were shadowy figures that we didn't pay attention to.

My thoughts would not be still. I should have changed my name when I came to Boston. When I'd arrived eight years ago, I thought about doing just that. People change their identities all the time, even stealing the names of dead people, but I had no idea how this was accomplished, so I didn't try. I certainly hadn't put my name out there on any dating service. That was something I absolutely couldn't afford, and I don't mean financially. I tried to keep a low profile.

But not low enough, apparently.

I helped a woman buy piano music for her daughter and I showed a country musician our array of acoustic guitars, but I couldn't keep the shakiness out of my knees. I kept having to sit down and rub my temples. And I kept looking toward the door. If Mudd was alive, as I was beginning to believe, would I recognize him if he walked in? I was sure I would.

His face always looked stubbly. And he was never without a dirty pork-pie hat made out of some material that I've heard referred to as houndstooth, which he wore on his sort-of shaved head. None of us had any idea where it came from. Once I asked him—the corner of his mouth went up and all he said was that it was his trademark. Yes, there would be no doubt. I would recognize him if he walked through that door.

Just before noon, Paige called the store. Greg was in the hospital.

"What?"

"Lilly, it's okay. He just broke his wrist. And we're thanking the Lord it wasn't more serious. They're putting some sort of a splint on it. He'll be home by the afternoon. He asked me to call you."

I didn't think there was any such thing as a non-serious break. "How did it happen?" I was talking to her on the store phone which was just behind the cash register. I wished I'd taken it elsewhere. A few customers were eyeing me curiously.

"Oh, it's this old building," Paige was saying. "I'm all for shutting down the office wing until the construction work is done. The board wants to. I don't know why we haven't done it. We're talking about moving into the gym until the work is complete."

I brushed my bangs out of my eyes. She wasn't answering my question. "But how did he break his wrist?"

"It was that carpet of his. You know, the one with the roads? He stepped on it and, unbeknownst to him, the boards directly beneath it had been removed."

I leaned forward on the counter on my forearms. Fortunately no customers were lined up at that moment to pay for things. "So, you're telling me he fell through the boards in his floor all the way to the basement?"

"No, oh no," she said. "That wouldn't happen—the floor joists are too close together. His leg went through, but the edges of the carpet caught on the floor on either side. And when he put his arm out to steady himself, he landed hard on his wrist. But it could have been much worse. He could have broken his leg."

"And he's okay?" Was this somehow my fault? Was he was so upset about us that he wasn't looking where he was going and walked right into a hole? "He's in the hospital now?"

"Dave and Henry are with him. I imagine they'll be taking him home soon."

"What about his conference?"

"Oh, he swears he's still going to that."

"I'll go over there," I said. "As soon as I can."

After we hung up, I straightened a few things on the counter with trembling fingers and prayed for Greg. Was I supposed to go and see him? Would he even want me to? He hadn't called me. He had instructed Paige to. What did that mean? I rang up a few orders and tried to keep a smile on my face while I kept looking at the clock.

Half an hour later, my morning shift was done and I raced to the hospital, parked and went inside. I had no idea where to find him, but after several hopelessly wrong detours and long treks down wrong hallways, I found him sitting on a bed in a treatment room, a plastic splint on his wrist and his arm in a sling. Henry and Dave were at his side. They were joking, smiling. How could they smile when he could have died?

"Greg!" I called, rushing over to him. "Are you okay?"

He managed a bit of a lopsided grin and said, "Hi, Lilly. I'm okay." He looked pale. His normally scruffy hair was matted on his forehead. He was in his jeans, and a loose white T-shirt. He was hugging his left arm to his chest.

"How did it happen?" My hands were shaking and I was barely able to catch my breath.

He must've seen the fear on my face, because right away he told me it wasn't serious.

"But, but…" I stammered. "How?"

He told me he'd gotten in that morning and had no idea that the workers had been removing the actual boards from the floor of his office. He stepped on his rug, and whoosh, away he fell. "Oh, Greg," I said. "I'm so sorry. Paige said it could have been worse. Like you could have broken your leg."

"God was watching out for you," Henry said.

I was trembling, shaking, and I just couldn't stop. "Are you in pain?" I asked.

He shrugged. "Not much."

Without thinking I reached out and touched his good arm. His skin was cool, clammy. I expected him to pull away or flinch but he didn't.

"When do you go home?" I asked. I kept my hand on his arm.

"In a few minutes, actually. They've gone to get a wheelchair."

"Do you want me to stay with you?"

"Whatever you want, Lilly," he said evenly. "Whatever you want."

EIGHT

I stayed with Greg until an orderly came with a wheel-chair. By the time I left the hospital, my music class was half over. But that was okay with me. I would go home; I didn't want to see my friends. I had too much on my mind and I knew that both Tiff and Neil would be all over me, asking how Greg liked the CD and wanting to see my engagement ring. Not only was I still not engaged, but Mudd had sent me five hundred and thirteen e-mails and the man I loved didn't want to be with me and had someone else call me when he went to the hospital.

Back in my apartment, I got out my guitar and sat on the edge of my bed. Playing normally relaxed me, usually connected me to God even, but today it wasn't working. What if Greg had fallen through the floor, despite those floor joists? He could've died. The thought brought tears to my eyes. I put my guitar away and paced through the apartment. I stopped at the kitchen window and looked out at the piles of dirt in the back, at the upended flowers, at the rip in the chain-link fence. Like my life, I thought—ripped up, the flowers torn out.

There was a meeting that evening at Paige and Henry's, which I sort of dreaded, but I was still the co-organizer of the youth group's fall cleanup, and even though what I felt like doing was burying myself in my bed, I had no choice but to show my face.

When I arrived at their house in the evening, the five of them—Paige, Henry, Sara and her two younger brothers—were still at the table finishing up a spaghetti dinner. The table was laden with spaghetti dishes, rolls and a salad bowl with a few remnants of green adhering to the bottom.

"You're here early," Sara piped up.

"You want some spaghetti?" the smaller of the two freckle-nosed boys asked me. A year apart in age, Sara's two brothers sat next to each other on one side of the table, napkins tucked into their collars, looking like mirror images.

"There's some left," said the other.

Then they looked at each other and giggled.

I was momentarily confused as I stood in the doorway and looked at my watch.

"The meeting wasn't scheduled until seven-thirty," Paige said softly. "But have a seat. With everything that's happened today, we had a late start to supper tonight. I'll make coffee in a minute. Did you get to see Greg?" she asked.

I nodded.

She shook her head. "It could have been so much worse."

Henry was at the far end of the table. His deep blue golf shirt made me think of Greg and my heart seemed to miss a beat. Henry got up and clapped his hands. "Okay, guys, take your plates to the counter and then let's go get to that homework."

Sara and Paige started quickly clearing the table. Except for the sprinkling of freckles, they did not look like they came from the same family. Sara was tall, slender and brown-haired; Paige was shorter, sturdier and light-haired.

Sara began filling the coffeepot.

"Make sure it's decaf," Paige called. Then she said to me, "The newest wrinkle in this whole thing is that now the workers are denying it." She loaded the dishwasher while she talked. "That's why we're so late. We had a meeting with the board. Dave spoke with the foreman, who has no idea why those boards were removed. That part of the floor was never supposed to be taken up. They are trying to get to the bottom of it."

I sat down at the kitchen table, watching the coffee filter through. I hummed softly as I tried to sort out my thoughts.

Sara got out mugs, while Paige finished with the dishwasher.

She wiped her hands on a towel and said, "But we can't dwell on it. Greg is fine." When the coffee was ready, Paige said, "Lilly, you said you were working on a new song?"

I nodded.

"Did you bring it along? Since we have a bit of time, maybe we could go over it before everyone comes."

Sara's eyes widened. "Can I hear it, too?"

I dug the lyrics and music out of my bag. After we poured our coffees, we went into the living room and I sat down at her grand piano.

"I don't have my guitar with me," I explained, "and I'm better on the guitar than the piano, but this'll give you the gist of it anyway."

"You sell yourself short," Paige said. "You have a natural music talent, guitar or piano. Most people have to work and work at the piano, but it seems to come naturally to you."

I tried a tentative chord progression and Paige asked, "How are the piano lessons coming along, anyway?"

"Fine. I'm enjoying them. I took them as a kid, so I've already got the basics."

"You're always singing. Do you know you're always singing, Lilly?" Sara asked.

I smiled. I'd been told that before. By Moira. A long time ago in another life.

"If I get my guitar," Sara said, "you could teach me the chords and I could play along, couldn't I?"

"Sure," I said.

By the time she was back, I was playing and singing through the first verse of my new worship song. By the second verse, Sara was strumming along. By the third verse, everyone was singing.

But when I got to the bridge, I could see Paige shaking her head. I stopped, pulled my fingers away from the keys and looked at her.

"Paige?" How stupid of me to sing this hopelessly unfinished and amateurish song for our church's professional music director who had an MA in music ministry. But Paige surprised me.

"You are an amazing songwriter, Lilly. You have a true gift from God, a true calling. A true calling. Amazing," she said. Paige, normally very reserved, had never given me a compliment like that before.

"A calling?" I had never thought of my music in precisely those terms before.

She nodded. And then she scooted onto the bench beside me and said, "Let's have a listen to that last phrase again. Play that last part for me, just before you say you don't know where it should go."

I did. By the end of it, Cinni had arrived and was leaning against the piano singing along, too, with her lovely voice.

I stopped again. "Don't you think it needs another verse here?"

"Actually, I don't," Paige said. "I like the way it ends. We could go back and repeat the first verse, but I don't think it needs anything else."

"You don't?"

"I don't."

The four of us sang through it a few more times, refining, polishing, adding a slightly different chord progression to the bridge.

Paige said, "How would it be if we introduced it in church on Sunday? It goes perfectly with Dave's sermon."

I couldn't believe it. "So you really think it's good enough the way it is?"

"I do."

We sang it through once more. When I looked up,

Greg was sitting there, one arm in a sling and the other hand on his knee. He was careful not to look at me. His hair looked like he had just walked in from a windstorm and he wore a Boston Red Sox T-shirt which I hadn't seen in a long time.

"Greg!" I said when we'd finished, trying to keep my voice light. "What're you doing here? Shouldn't you be home?"

"She's right," Paige said. "No way should you be here. Aren't you in pain?"

"A bit, but this is much better than staying home and not doing anything."

"Staying home and resting, you mean?" Paige said.

"How did you get here?" I asked. "Please tell us you didn't drive."

"Cinni's dad was kind enough to pick me up on the way."

I stayed seated on the piano bench during the meeting, stealing glances at Greg. Once, our eyes locked. He turned away first, but not before a shadow of sadness drifted across his face. Was he sad because of us, or was he just in physical pain?

As I sat there while Cinni and Sara unveiled the computer spreadsheet they had developed, a dark thought that had been lurking in the back of my mind finally came to the surface. I almost gasped aloud when I thought of it. What if Greg's accident wasn't an accident?

Later that evening, my father called and told me that the man who'd phoned claimed to be someone from my old high school wanting to tell me about a reunion.

"My class reunion was last year," I said.

"I wondered about that. The whole thing seemed very fishy. When I wouldn't give him your e-mail, he got angry and said it was very important. I said, 'Not on your life.' I told him he could leave his name and number but he hung up on me."

"Thanks, Dad. I'm glad you didn't give it to him, and if anyone calls in the future, please don't."

"I won't. You can count on that. There are too many undesirable people out there."

We talked a while longer. I missed my dad and I told him I'd try to schedule a trip home soon.

"You do that. I know it doesn't always seem so, and she may not say anything, but your mother really misses you. She talks about you all the time, Lilly. She's very proud of you, of what you've made of your life now."

"She is?"

"Yes, she is."

Then why didn't she ever tell me that? I wanted to ask. But I didn't. We said goodbye and I joined Bridget in our living room. Popcorn was popping in the microwave and she was watching a movie and knitting, as per usual. She aimed the remote and muted the TV when I sat down on the couch.

She wanted to know all about Greg's accident and how I was feeling, so I told her.

"It's so weird," she said, "that that little piece of rug happened to be placed just so, and that he didn't see that the floor underneath had been torn up."

"Weird," I agreed.

I told her what Dave had said about the workers

denying it, and she shook her head. "So what did the police say?"

"The police?" I looked at her in confusion.

"Yes. What did the police say?"

"As far as I know, nobody called the police about it," I said. "I don't think it was a police matter. It was just a construction accident."

She sighed deeply and stared at me. "Lilly, you went to the police right? About Mudd and the stalking? And the e-mails you got? That's what I'm talking about. So, what did they say?"

Ah. Another classic Bridget topic change. "I didn't get a chance. With all that happened to Greg today I just totally forgot."

"But you're going to, right?" The microwave dinged and she got up and poured the popcorn into a big bowl.

"I will. What are you knitting?" I said, attempting to move the conversation away from the police.

"A sweater." She put the bowl down on the counter and flexed her fingers before picking it back up. "For my niece for Christmas."

"You have a few months."

"I know, but after this I want to do a scarf and mittens for my little nephew." Popcorn bowl in hand, she went and stood beside the window and said thoughtfully, "I went over there and buzzed and buzzed, but there was no answer."

I was bewildered again by the change of subject. "Buzzed what?"

"At Mrs. Eberline's."

"I'm sure she's okay, Bridget. Seriously." The sturdy

little woman who'd come traipsing into the apartment that day looked like someone who could take care of herself.

But Bridget only shrugged as she stood by the window eating handfuls of popcorn.

NINE

I have three guitar students: Paige and Henry's daughter Sara, nice Irma who bakes me things and a man named Ted who looks to be a taller and more emaciated version of what I imagine Ichabod Crane might look like. Ted came to me by way of Neil—he is Neil's downstairs neighbor. According to Neil, Ted asked if he would mind "tutoring him in the art of the guitar." Those were his words. Neil said he was too busy with course work and recommended me. Unlike Irma who I feel a rapport with, and Sara who I love, Ted is very quiet and I never quite know what he is thinking.

He is forty-ish, almost bald with sparse brown hair and wears a large pair of glasses which look like leftovers from the '70s. Today he had on a white shirt rolled up at the elbows and faded polyester pants. Ted drives a pizza delivery truck in the evenings which leaves his mornings free for other pursuits such as music lessons and an astronomy class which he audits at my college. He has zero musical talent and tends to strum the strings at the same heavy volume on all songs.

He played, all skeletal fingers on the fret board as he tried to get through a simple chord progression for "My Bonnie Lies Over the Ocean." I tried to be patient with him. I tried to concentrate on teaching, but I kept thinking of Greg and Mudd and the five hundred and thirteen e-mails that I'd received.

After I bid adieu to Ted, I saw that someone had left a text message on my cell phone. It was from Paige.

Can't send you e-mail without it bouncing. Praise practice tonight in new church basement @ 7. Bring new song. Call if you can't make it.

Ah, yes. I hadn't given Paige my new e-mail address.

Tonight? It wasn't our regular practice night, but it was good to keep busy. I'd be there.

The front door of the church was unlocked when I arrived that evening and the lights were on. There were no cars in the lot. Strange, I thought. Maybe I was early again. I rechecked the text message. Seven. I checked the time. Six-fifty. I wasn't that early. But lately my brain has been so frazzled I could have easily come on the wrong day. I felt a little uneasy as I opened the door. My fears were put to rest when I heard the unmistakable sound of Paige at the piano, playing one of my favorite worship songs. I sang along with it as I entered. This was a good thing. The church could get spooky at night. It was a building I did not want to be alone in. I thought about Greg's accident and shuddered.

I headed down the hall toward the staircase and immediately encountered yellow caution tape and a sawhorse blocking the hallway. The entire floor had been torn up and carted away.

The only way to proceed would be to walk along a series of staggered two-by-sixes which had been laid across the floor joists. When I was a little girl I prided myself on my ability to balance on a log, but with guitar case in hand, I didn't feel like crawling my way across the boards. I could end up tumbling down into the basement. How could we even have church here when it's like this?

"Paige!" She didn't hear me.

I leaned over the barricade and tried to see through to the basement. While I couldn't see much, I could tell that the basement was lit and the music was coming from down there. I was anxious to see how they'd turned that dingy basement up into a practice room.

"Hey! How do I get down there?"

I decided to go back out the front door and walk around the building. If I came in the back way, I could get down to the basement by the backstairs. By now, I knew those stairs by heart.

I exited, and made my way around the brightly lit church. The back was dark and I trudged through brittle weeds. A cold wind blew and I held my jacket to my chin and clutched my bagful of music. My guitar case slapped against my knees in the wind.

In the spillover parking lot, one seldom used, I saw a van half hidden by scrawny bushes. It looked like Stuart's, but I couldn't be sure. Stuart usually attends our praise practice to coordinate the projection system with the words of the songs. He was probably in the basement working with Paige, the two of them so engrossed in what they're doing that they couldn't hear me. The fact that he'd parked way back here indicated that he'd already tried the front door and knew the hallway wasn't navigable.

I tried the seldom-used back door. Unlocked. I went inside. The light was on, but I was in an unfamiliar part of the church. The old building was filled with many winding halls and tiny rooms. Even though I'd gone to this church for eight years, there were still places in the building I've never been to. This was one of them. I wandered down the echoey hallways, looking for the familiar backstairs, calling as I did so.

"Stuart? Paige?"

I would be lying if I said I wasn't beginning to get spooked. Even with the music playing, I was feeling rattled. I kept calling their names and getting no answer, while Paige just kept playing and playing.

I wandered down one unfamiliar hallway that twisted and turned. I opened up a door and a mop fell out and hit me on the head. I shrieked. Paige just kept on playing the piano. I righted the mop, closed the door and kept walking. Finally, I turned and was back in familiar territory. I breathed a sigh of relief. The steps were right in front of me. The door to the stairs was propped open, the lights were on downstairs and the piano was blaring. I headed down.

"Hey, you guys," I said as I descended. "So, the new practice room is down here. How cool…"

I got to the bottom, and above me the door slammed shut. That was my first clue that something was seriously wrong. The second was when I saw that the basement was not a renovated practice room. The place was filled with white dust, junk and debris, and the old rooms were still intact.

The third clue was that Paige's piano playing came from a small CD player set on a sawhorse, the volume cranked up to deafening levels. My knees gave way and I sagged against a near wall. I had just walked into a trap. The music had been the bait, and I'd been lured here. I reached and turned off the CD player. The lights went off, and I was plunged into silent darkness.

I needed to get out. I turned and tried to find the stairs in the dark, my guitar case bumping wildly and noisily against my knees, and against the walls on either side of me.

I can't say I was surprised when I finally got to the top of the stairs and found that the door was locked. I shoved at it. I banged on it. I shouted, but it remained firmly locked. I leaned against the door, gasping, barely able to breathe, and got out my cell phone. No service. I banged on the door again, but of course it wouldn't budge. I started shaking so badly that I dropped my guitar case and it clattered against the wall. I sat down on the top step, put my head in my hands in the pitch black and tried to think. Mudd was no longer a nightmare from my past who might or might not be dead and who was sending me e-mails from some distant location. Mudd was alive and Mudd was here. Right now.

It was Mudd who had removed Greg's floorboards. Mudd had tried to hurt Greg. Mudd, somehow, had easy access to this church. I stood up, screamed, banged and shouted. No one came. I kept trying my cell phone, but could find no service. Tears welled in my eyes. And I thought of Greg. Would I ever see him again? Would I ever get to tell him how sorry I was about everything? Would I ever get to tell him about my past? Would I ever get to tell him again that I loved him?

I sat on the step for a few moments in the darkness, realizing that I only had one option. I had to go back down to the basement and try to find my way through the hallways to the opposite staircase. Once there, I could climb over the barrier and crawl along the two-by-sixes until I got to the front door. It would be a challenge, but what other choice did I have? Stay on the stairs until morning?

I proceeded slowly, using the light from my cell phone screen. It wasn't much, but it was better than nothing. The dank air caught in my nostrils. Halfway down the steps I remembered that I had a little flashlight on my keychain. I fumbled in my bag and found it. I aimed it down the steps. Much better than the phone.

At the bottom, I'd try to find a light switch. That would be my first priority. When I got there, I flicked the switch. Nothing. No light. I tried it again and again, hoping it would turn on, but no matter how many times I tried, the basement remained in blackness.

Holding my guitar case firmly, I made my way slowly across the debris-filled basement with my little light as quietly as I could. I needed to listen. I needed to get across the basement quickly, one step in front of the next. I heard a slight scratching behind me from the bathroom. I stopped. Froze. It was gone.

I panicked. I needed to get to those far steps as fast as I could. But in my haste I bumped into a metal folding chair which clanged as it fell across a piece of piping. The noise was ear-splitting in the dark and I groaned. My guitar case clunked against the cement floor and from within came the sonorous sound of the strings.

I stepped over piles of nails and bumped into boards. I picked one up. Maybe I could use it as a weapon. My knees touched against a big pile of something soft. I shone my light on it. Insulation. I kept walking, picking my way through the torn-up halls. How could I have been so stupid? But the text message had come from Paige's phone. Did Mudd break into her house, find her phone and call mine? What if he'd done something to Paige, or Henry, or Sara, or the boys?

I aimed my light around me to get my bearings. To my left were square cubicle rooms filled with old chairs, desks and other junk which was piled aimlessly. Directly in front of me was what used to be a kitchen. There was an ancient fridge without a door, and a stove. Deep sinks lined one wall.

Behind me was an old bathroom with rusty fixtures. A door with a crooked mirror affixed to it was open and I jumped back when I saw my specter-like reflection in it.

I swung the light quickly away and tripped over a pile of boards, but caught myself before I went sprawling to the floor. I dropped my flashlight. It flickered, dimmed and went out. I got on hands and knees, and felt around for several minutes before I found it. It worked, but was decidedly dimmer. I squeezed it between my thumb and forefinger and it brightened again, but I knew its minutes were numbered. My hand trembled as I held it. I needed to get out.

God, help me make it to the staircase, I prayed. *God, please help me get out of here.*

I was trying desperately to remember how to get to the front stairs. I closed my eyes and pictured it. Around the corner, down the hall, turn right and the front staircase should be there. I'd been this way before. I felt like I was in one of those dreams where, no matter how fast you walk, you never make any headway, like wading through thick mud.

I hoped I was walking down the right hall. I thought I recognized a bunch of little rooms. Yes, this was correct. Now I just turn the corner and the stairs will be right there. I aimed my flashlight.

The staircase was gone.

Had I gotten that turned around down here? I backed up a bit. Then I directed my fading light to where I thought the staircase should be, and saw that I was in the right place but the stairs had been removed. Way up at the top of the wall, the door-sized hole was zigzagged with yellow caution tape. The stairs were truly gone. There was no way out. I was trapped.

Construction workers always have ladders, I thought. I'll find a ladder. But as I picked my way through the basement, I could find nothing that would work. Could I pile chairs up and get out? The door was way too high and I didn't trust myself in my shaky state to do it.

There was only one thing to do. Go back the way I came, and then kick my way out at the top of the stairs.

I'd exchange my wooden board for one of those metal pipes and smash it against the door. Cops did this on TV, didn't they? I could do it, too.

I started back. As I walked past one of the little rooms I spooked myself again, then I realized that the white ghostly form which towered over me was really just a pile of chairs covered in a white sheet. *Breathe,* I told myself.

I began down the hall again, coming to the old bathroom where I'd scared myself with my own reflection. I faced the bathroom mirror just to prove to myself that there was nothing to be afraid of. And then I saw him. He was there, staring at me from the shadows. I hadn't seen him for eight years, yet he seemed unchanged as he stood there looking at me.

Mudd.

I cried out and backed away against the wall, the tears coming fast and hard. "What do you want?" I sobbed. "I don't have your money! It's all gone! Stay away from me! Leave me alone!" I was frantic; I was shaking. But he continued to stare at me, unmoving, a hint of a smile on his face as he leaned casually against the bathroom door, that awful hat perched on his head.

He continued to look at me without saying a thing. There was an odd light about his face which made him look ghostlike. I turned and ran, hiding in the old kitchen behind a rusted stove—shivering, crouching, holding my guitar case in one hand and the board in another. There was no way out. He had me. I heard his footsteps. He was coming toward me, down the hall. He called my name.

"Lilly?"

Lilly? He usually called me Lil. I hoped my guitar case was hidden from view. I held tightly to the board.

I heard him walk into the kitchen. He had a very bright flashlight. When he came close to where I had hunkered down, I buried my face in my arms and screamed for him to go away. He reached for me, grabbing my collar. I kept my eyes closed and scrabbled away from him in the darkness, screaming, scratching, waving the board, doing anything I could. "Let go of me! I don't have what you want anymore! Let go!"

"Lilly!" He reached for my shoulders and held tight. "What's wrong, Lilly?"

Stuart? I wrenched out of his grasp and faced him. "Stuart! What are you doing here?" He was all in black, and in the darkness of the basement kitchen, all I could see was his face.

"I heard someone screeching like a banshee, so I came down here to find you hiding behind the stove. But more to the point, what are *you* doing here?"

"I came because…I got a text message…from Paige…about a practice…music…here…" My words were coming out in gasping sobs. Stuart may be here now, but Mudd was also down here. "Mudd," I said. "He's down here, Stuart. He tried to kill Greg. We have to get out of here."

"There's no one down here but us, Lilly. What are you talking about?"

"But I saw…out there." I pointed. "Someone's in the hall. By the bathroom."

"Where?"

I didn't want to go back to the mirror, but I did and

there he was, smirking at us from the bathroom. Stuart calmly walked toward the unmoving Mudd and tore the picture from the mirror. "You mean this guy?" he said.

A *photograph?* "But I thought…it looked so real. The first time I looked over there, I saw my own face in the mirror," I explained. "I remember that, because it scared the living daylights out of me. And then later Mudd was there."

"Mudd?"

"That's his name."

"You know this guy?" He tapped his finger on the photo.

I nodded. "I used to. I knew him a long time ago." I eyed him.

He turned the picture over. "The picture looks pretty old."

I peered at it. It was a photo I recognized, one taken just before I left. "But he was here," I said. "He put this picture up."

"Well, *somebody* did."

"*He* did. He came down here and put up that picture to try to scare me. And it worked." I looked at him. "How did you get down here anyway?"

"By the only staircase that's viable, the back one. But there was a chair wedged against the door."

"A chair? There was a chair there?"

"It seemed pretty weird," Stuart said.

"Where were you? Why were you here?"

"In the sanctuary. In the projection booth. We just got some new software and I was getting used to it."

As we made our way down the narrow hallways, I

told Stuart how Paige had text messaged me, how as soon as I'd arrived, I'd heard the music and how I'd gotten trapped in the basement.

"Did you hear Paige playing the piano?" I asked.

"Vaguely. I just thought she was practicing somewhere. I didn't think much about it."

"Well, this is where the music came from." I showed him the portable CD player.

"We'd better get out of here," Stuart said.

"Good idea."

He carried my guitar case, and stayed close to me as we made our way up the stairs. Even though I was a little uncomfortable with Stuart, being with him was sure better than the alternative.

"When we get upstairs, we'll call the police. Cell phone reception's lousy down here," he said.

"So I've noticed."

"And then we'll go to my van. It's out back. I had to park it out there because of the construction. We probably shouldn't wait in the church."

"Fine by me."

His van was big and dirty, the inside an echoey metal shell with a few seats that looked as though they had been added after the van had been purchased. He had to brush empty coffee cups and gum wrappers from the front passenger seat before there was room for me to sit down.

I was shivering uncontrollably, so he turned the engine on and the heat. I kept glancing at the church while we waited for the police to arrive. I asked him about Hotmail accounts and he said it was pretty impossible to figure out where they originated, but if I wanted him to, he could have a look. I thought about it, and realized, why bother? I already knew who sent the e-mails, and I knew where he was.

I could tell that Stuart wanted to know about Mudd, but I didn't want to share anything else with him. At one point, I began to wonder how much I really knew about Stuart. He wore black. So did Mudd. He shaved his head. So did Mudd. He had a faint dark moustache. So did Mudd. Come to think of it, the resemblance between them was a little creepy.

And now here I was, in his van on a dark night. I only had his word that he'd actually called the police. "Did you call the police?" I asked.

He nodded and looked around him. "They're a little slow sometimes."

"They should be here soon?"

"Right."

"How long did they say?" I squirmed on my seat, wondering if I should open the door and flee.

"Five minutes."

"Five minutes? It's been more than five minutes."

He looked over at me. "Lilly, they'll be here soon. Don't worry. The police will come, they'll find them."

"Him."

"Okay, him."

Just then, a police cruiser came slowly around the back. Stuart flicked his high beams and they drove over. The two officers who emerged could not have been more different. The man was gigantic, probably six-six with broader shoulders than most linebackers and a large-featured, rubbery-looking face. He introduced himself as Roy. The woman with him was teensy, blond and fine-featured. For someone so delicate, the woman, who introduced herself as Jackie, had a surprisingly deep and husky voice. It sounded like a smoker's voice.

They wanted to hear what happened before they checked the church. Between the two of us we got out the story. Jackie asked all the questions while Roy sat and listened, writing it all down.

They took the picture of Mudd and asked us the same questions in many different ways. Who was this man? Where did we get this picture? Did one of us bring it in with us?

"Is this your picture?" they kept asking me.

I kept shaking my head. It wasn't my picture. But yes, I knew this man from a long time ago. The officers wrote down the whole story as I talked. I told them that the man was someone from my past. He'd threatened me then and he was threatening me again, now. It felt odd to be telling my story in front of Stuart and not Greg. Why couldn't it have been Greg who found me?

They asked about the music, and we told them we'd left the CD player in the basement. Finally they let us go, saying that they were calling in a number of other officers to help look through the church.

As I went home, I realized that I hadn't told them about the e-mails.

TEN

His long fingers were in my hair, playing with the ends of it, splaying it out across his palm. I wanted him to stop, needed him to stop, but I was powerless. The feel of his callused hands running through my hair—strand by strand by strand by strand—was hypnotic. And I was falling under his spell again. Cigarettes were on his breath and he talked to me gently, quietly, but insistently.

It was such a real sensation, those fingers in my hair, that I actually stopped playing my guitar and waved my left hand across my head as if shooing away a pesky fly. I had to remind myself that this was Sunday morning and I was in my best dress, standing on the platform of my church teaching my new song to the congregation. I looked out to see their singing, joyous faces. He could be sitting down there, even now, watching me. Maybe he was behind a post, or in the shadows where I couldn't see him, wearing all black the way he always did, observing me, ready to pounce on my faults, ready to tell me afterward that I'd messed up—that I'd messed up, that I'd messed up, messed up, messed up. I put my hands back on the guitar strings and began strumming along in time to the song.

I had dared to hope that it was over. But it was far from over. The police had called me at home the night it happened. They hadn't found anyone in the church, although they'd spent hours searching. Dave and Henry had been summoned, and a few other church board members, but the search had yielded nothing. They came to the apartment. They questioned me further. The CD player that had blared Paige's music turned out to be Bridget's. Her name and address were on the back. I was shocked. She was surprised, too, claiming she didn't even know it was missing. She got up to check. Sure enough, the CD player she kept in the top of her closet was gone. Had Mudd actually been in the apartment? I put my hand to my mouth and choked as horror rose up in my throat.

The police had started grilling me at that point. Did I know about her CD player? Had I taken it to the church to use? Did I know how it got there? I told them I had no idea, but they didn't seem to believe me. They asked me over and over about the photo. I kept telling them it wasn't my photo, but they kept asking. It was as if they thought I had taken it with me to the church, along with Bridget's CD player, and that I had done all of this to get attention.

"Why do you keep asking me these questions?" I'd said to them.

"Ms. Johnson, the man in the photo, Michael Binderson, is dead. We ran his name through the system."

"That's what he wants everyone to think. He's not dead."

"He died eight years ago. He was shot once in the head, and the person responsible, a Mark Pelsar, is currently in prison for his murder."

"He's alive. He faked his death. He's here. I know he is," I'd said.

The sound of singing brought me back to the church. I looked ahead to where Stuart was bent over the projector and sound system. Maybe Mudd had somehow won Stuart's confidence, convinced him that I was nuts, that instead of Mudd being obsessed with me, it was the other way around. Did Stuart think I was obsessed with Mudd and that I had done all of this to get attention? After all, the CD player was Bridget's, and who had more access to her stuff than me? My mind started to spin off in crazy directions.

What if Mudd was, even now, not only in the church but at the controls of my microphone? That thought sent waves of panic up my spine. I choked on a word and hoped nobody noticed. I had to concentrate on my breathing and my singing. I looked up and out through the large, hexagonal, stained glass window on the back wall behind Stuart. It was a picture that always gave me hope—Christ who is the Lamb, carrying a lamb in his arms. Yet I felt not hopeful, but hopeless.

I scanned the congregation. There in the front row was Greg sitting in a middle of a group of boys. Kids love Greg. They cluster around him. And now with his cast and sling, he was the center of attention. I looked away, feeling a tear well up in the corner of my eye.

Several rows behind him and to the right was Bridget who was seated at the end of a row. Behind her was a row of elderly women. And over to the left, surprisingly, I saw Neil and Tiff. How nice that they came. I'd invited them often enough—I'm glad they finally took me up on it. When Neil saw me looking at him, he smiled.

Sometime during the hour, it had started to rain and it was as if someone had gradually dimmed the lights. The stained glass became colorless, almost gray. I looked down at my music.

We were on the second verse of my song now, the verse which asks the question: *Where is God in this life of mine?* When I wrote this song, I wasn't asking that question, not really. I had all the answers then. My past was safely buried and it would never bother me. It would never be unearthed. It would never haunt me.

Now, as I sang, I wondered: *Is* God in any of this? I saw a shadow move underneath the stained glass window. Or was that just the play of light and dark from outside, or a waving of tree branches?

High around the cornices of the church were tiny sculpted angels with their wings outspread. As I gazed at them, they seemed to morph into gargoyles with tongues and teeth and feral eyes. I wondered if the church held too many ancient secrets and that the act of renovation had been much like turning over a rock. Maybe we were disturbing old ghosts. How coincidental that this should happen at the church, when it was also happening in my life.

In front of me, just below Stuart's projection area in the balcony, rows and rows of happy singers stood clapping their hands to the music. I studied the balcony, thinking of a terrible story Greg had told me about a child who fell to her death from that balcony a hundred years ago. I could not look at the balcony this morning without thinking about that. I wondered what would happen if the balcony suddenly fell off its supports and plunged to ground level. It was as if everywhere I looked, the church taunted me with rain and darkness, death and evil.

We were singing the chorus of my song in which the word praise is repeated four times. I *wanted* to praise God. I wanted all of the bad things to be once and for all defeated so I could really praise God. And then I heard Mudd's voice. *"Lil,"* he said. Just one word, my name. He was calling me through my monitor. His voice was so clear to me that I stopped singing for a moment. I looked over at Paige on the keyboards. She frowned at me slightly. Had she heard it, too? Probably not. This was my own demon. Like all the church staff, she knew what had happened the other night. The police had spoken with her. Her phone showed no record of the text message that night. I showed the police my phone with the message, but they believed I had somehow put the message on myself. I have no idea how I would even do that, I told them. But they just looked at me.

"Lil." I heard it again.

Was Mudd up there with Stuart? Had he broadcast "Lil" on my monitor only? No, don't be ridiculous. I must be hearing things…

"Your hair could be black, you know. That would work. Black and straight. I know someone who could do that."

I had looked up at him, at his dark eyes milky from too many drugs, and pulled my head away from his groping fingers. "No," I'd said. "I don't want it black. I want to keep it the color it is."

He smirked at me, tipped his hat at a more jaunty angle and said, "You forget something. If I say it will be black, then it will be black." And he leaned toward me. "Because I own you. I own you. I own you. I own you, I own you, I own you, I own you." He repeated it over and over, like a scratched CD stuck on the same note.

A loud riff on the bass guitar snapped me once again to the present. I kept singing while the gargoyles taunted me from the cornices. I decided I had merely imagined my name being called.

I had no right being up here, leading the congregation in song. I was not a good person. I'd stolen from Mudd. That could almost be forgiven, but stealing from Moira—that was unforgivable.

The prayer over, I made my way down to the sanctuary. There was one awkward moment when one of the teen girls got up to let me slide in beside Greg. Greg looked up at me. Was that hope in his eyes, hope that I would sit there? No, I thought, I'm not good enough for Greg. I looked away from him, my heart in pieces. The girl sat back down, puzzled, when I moved in to sit beside Bridget instead. Bridget squeezed my arm and smiled. I felt so close to tears that I bent my head forward so my hair would cover my face.

All during Dave's sermon, I found myself thinking about Moira. Maybe I needed to make things right with her. Maybe she would know about Mudd. I checked my calendar in my head. I could leave as early as Thursday. I'd have to talk to Neil, Tiff and Lora—we were making headway on our music history project, and I owed it to them not to skip out. Plus, I had music students. But if I rescheduled them, I could leave on Thursday and, if all went well, I could be back by Saturday night. If a ticket was available.

I had a Visa card that I was careful to pay off each month—some of my mother's financial advice had rubbed off—so there would be no problem booking a plane ticket. I knew where Moira lived. All these years and she still lived in that same little house in New Orleans. I'd looked up the address on Google Earth after Katrina to make sure it was still standing. It was, and she was still listed. She'd be there. I knew that.

Dear God, what should I do?

Dave was praying the benediction, and I realized that I hadn't listened to a word he'd preached. I rose with the others, moving quickly up to the platform to collect my music. I'd drop it off in Paige's office, get myself home and look online for that ticket.

ELEVEN

I was putting my guitar into its case following the service when Stuart came over, a bunch of mikes and cords draped over his arm.

"Are you okay, Lilly?" His voice was soft, almost apologetic.

"Fine," I said. I snapped the case shut and stood up. When we were facing each other, he said, "I wanted you to know something. I don't know if the police believe you or not, but I want you to know that I believe you."

Stuart was considerably taller than Greg. It felt odd to have to look up so far to meet a man's eyes. His dark eyes were bright as he looked at me.

"And the reason I know you were telling the truth is that I saw how scared you were down there."

"Thank you," I said. I picked up my guitar case. "Thanks for believing me." I paused, then cocked my head. "Stuart, do you know if it's possible to send someone a message on your cell phone and make it appear it came from somewhere else?"

"You're thinking about the text message you got."

I nodded. "The police think I put it on my phone myself. Apparently, there's a way to do that. But they never even suggested that *someone else* could've sent me a text message, making it appear to come from another phone."

"That's possible, too," he said.

"I didn't send myself a message."

"I know you didn't."

"And I didn't steal Bridget's CD player and bring it to the church. But Mudd would do something like that. That's exactly the sort of thing he would do. He's an evil person."

"I'm sorry you're afraid, Lilly."

"I am afraid. But I'd like to see him. I want to confront him."

"Be careful."

I promised I would. "And, Stuart, thanks for being there and helping me. I don't know what would have happened if you hadn't been there."

He smiled, gathered up the mikes and cords and we parted.

Bridget was in the foyer. "Don't wait for me," I told her. "I have to drop this stuff off in Paige's office."

She gave my arm a little squeeze. "I'm going home to change and then to my parents for lunch. Are you going to be okay?"

"Don't worry about me," I said. "I've got so much catch-up work to do this afternoon. I'm so behind." In the past few days I'd let my classes slide, and my piano, too. I needed to get my life back on track.

"We'll have a good talk when I get back tonight. I'll see you later," she said.

Her face was so earnest, and I wanted to tell her right then, *"Bridget, I'm not a good person, I'm not a good friend. I'll only let you down. I had a good friend once, and I betrayed her. Stay away from me. You'd be wise to just keep your distance."*

Getting myself to Paige's office to drop off the music meant walking right by Greg's door. It was open, but he wasn't there. I'd actually hoped that nobody would be there—not Greg nor Paige. It would suit me just fine to leave the music in the box outside her door and then scurry home to buy that plane ticket.

Paige's door was ajar, however, and there she was, standing beside the file cabinet shuffling sheets of music, skinny glasses down on the end of her nose, gray-blond hair behind her ears. She looked up when she heard me approach. "Lilly, come on in. How are you feeling?"

"I'm okay," I said.

Her coral lips formed themselves into a thin line. "You seemed a bit, I don't know, *distracted* up there this morning, Lilly. Are you sure you're okay? You've been through a lot."

"I'm okay, really."

"That was quite a scare you had the other night."

"I've had an awful couple of weeks."

"I understand," Paige said. Paige is one of the few people who remembers what I was like when I first came to Boston. Most in this large church would not remember me from then at all. Both Dave and Greg had come on to the ministerial staff after I'd cleaned up my act. If the church people recalled anything about me, they would remember a dark-haired girl with many piercings. I was tough and hard then.

"Thank you," I said, my voice hoarse. "Thanks for doing so much for me through the years."

I heard steps in the hallway and Greg poked his head in. "Paige, I wanted to get your opinion on—" And then he saw me. It was a moment before he said, "Great song, Lilly, your new one. It sounded nice."

"Thank you. How's your wrist?" I asked.

"Oh." He looked down at it. "It's not bad. More of a nuisance now than anything."

I kept my gaze averted, while Greg told Paige he'd touch base with her the following morning.

After he left, Paige said, "Greg is right. Your song is beautiful, and all the more so knowing the struggles you've been through."

"I still think it needs a last verse," I said. Then I told her, "I'm thinking I might be going away for a few days at the end of the week. I thought I'd let you know, in case you needed me for anything. There's a person I have to see."

She raised her eyebrows, but I didn't offer any explanation. I told her I'd see her next week, and left her office. I thought for sure Greg would have been long gone by now, but his door stood open and as I walked past, he said, "Lilly?" I turned to see him sitting at his desk. "Can we talk for a minute?"

Wordlessly, I entered his extremely messy, torn-up office. The far wall was still gone and the dismal light from the window made his office look like an entrance to a cave. The hole in the floor he had fallen into had been covered with rough plywood. There were half-filled boxes all around.

He saw where my gaze had settled and said, "The foreman still says his guys didn't do this. I'm not even supposed to be here. I'm supposed to have cleaned all this out already and be working in the gym."

"That might be a good idea."

"The bad news is that I can't pack with only one arm, but the good news is that I've got a whole pile of kids in the youth group who have offered to help me tomorrow."

"That's nice." I was feeling awkward, wondering what I could say to Greg, how much I could tell him. I desperately wanted to tell him everything, but once again I couldn't make myself do it.

"I heard about what happened to you in the basement," he said.

I sighed. "It was horrible."

I looked at the planes of his face now, the way his eyes crinkled when he talked. A chunk of hair on the left side of his head stuck straight up. I wanted to touch it, to smooth it down. His expression now was soft, but I kept remembering how distant he was at the restaurant, the way we'd spent the entire evening talking about nothing. I heard Paige exit her office and close the door, her high heels click-clacking as she went down the hall. We didn't say anything until we could no longer hear her. Then Greg suddenly became serious.

"I want to apologize for the other night at Primo's."

He looked down at his desk. "I'd had a sort of strange day. It was just…I don't know. I had a lot on my mind. I was working through some things and ended up taking it out on you." He looked up at me. "Did you ever feel like you had your whole life planned out and you're happy and God is blessing you and life is good, and then suddenly—you don't know how it happened—but you're on this other road? Like you've been on a super-highway and then without warning, you're driving down this country road and you don't know how you got there, and it's dark and you're lost?"

I nodded. He was thinking about his first wife, I could tell. I knew exactly what he meant, however, and told him I did.

"But that was still no excuse for how I acted."

"It's okay." I looked into his blue eyes, watched how he ran his hand over his head, noted the way he sighed and shifted to his other foot. These were all things I loved about Greg. When I didn't say anything more, he said, "I've got a lot on my mind."

I looked away from him, struggling for words, and my eyes landed on the corner of his desk where a CD cover was sticking out from under a stack of papers.

He said, "I wanted to say I'm sorry because I'm leaving tomorrow for that youth conference I've been telling you about. I wanted to clear this up and apologize before I went."

"Even with your wrist, you're still going?"

"It doesn't hurt anymore. I can even drive. It could've been so much worse. I got off easy."

We sat in awkward silence for a moment.

Get 2 Books FREE!

Steeple Hill Books,
publisher of inspirational fiction, presents

Love Inspired.
SUSPENSE

A SERIES OF EDGE-OF-YOUR-SEAT SUSPENSE NOVELS

FREE BOOKS!
Get two free books by acclaimed, inspirational authors!

FREE GIFTS!
Get two exciting surprise gifts absolutely free!

2 FREE BOOKS

We'd like to send you two free books to introduce you to the Love Inspired® Suspense series. Your two books have a combined cover price of $11.00 in the U.S. and $13.00 in Canada, but they are yours free! We'll even send you two wonderful surprise gifts. You can't lose!

Each of your **FREE** books is filled with riveting inspirational suspense featuring Christian characters facing challenges to their faith... and their lives!

GET 2 FREE BOOKS!

HURRY!
Return this card today to get **2 FREE Books** *and* **2 FREE Bonus Gifts!**

Love Inspired.
SUSPENSE

YES! *Please send me the 2 FREE Love Inspired® Suspense books and 2 FREE gifts for which I qualify. I understand that I am under no obligation to purchase anything further, as explained on the back of this card.*

affix
free
books
sticker
here

323 IDL ERRT   123 IDL ERQ5

FIRST NAME   LAST NAME

ADDRESS

APT.#   CITY

STATE/PROV.   ZIP/POSTAL CODE

"Lilly, can I e-mail you when I get to Baltimore? Would that be all right?"

"I'd like that. I have a new e-mail," I said. I wrote it down on a scrap of paper and handed it to him.

He took the piece of paper and looked up at me quizzically.

"It's a long story. I got fed up with my service provider."

We were quiet for another minute and then he totally surprised me by saying, "I was thinking that today might be a good day for a picnic."

"Come again?"

"A picnic? You and me? Like we used to do on Sunday afternoons?"

I stared at him. Yes, we often did go on picnics. Sometimes we ate out, and sometimes I would go to his place and sample his cooking. But just as often, we'd grab sub sandwiches and head to the water, eating them while we watched the boats and the waves, trying to keep the gulls from flocking around our food.

"We could go to the picnic shelter by the seawall."

"You're serious," I said. I wanted to spend Sunday afternoon with this man more than anything in the world.

"Of course I'm serious," he said.

"But it's raining," I protested.

"When has a little rain ever stopped us?"

We were standing close together. He reached out and touched my face. I took a breath. He was going to kiss me. This afternoon I would tell him everything that I'd told Stuart. I moved toward him, bumped into his desk and knocked a little stack of papers, envelopes and books to the floor. As we both bent to pick up the fallen items, our hands touched. I started to laugh, but my laugh died in my throat as I looked down at the CD I was holding.

I recognized the photo on the front. It was one of the five hundred and thirteen e-mails I'd received. There was no identification on the front, just that picture. Had Greg listened to it? If he had, he would have immediately recognize my voice.

"What's this?" I tried to keep the trembling out of my voice.

"I have no idea. It came in the mail."

"You got it in the mail?"

He shrugged. "I haven't had a chance to really look at it yet. I'm thinking it might be some sort of promotional thing for a Christian rock group. Except there's no name or anything. Do you know who they are? You seem like you know them." Greg was watching me very carefully.

"This girl looks like she's part of a Christian rock group?"

He took the CD from my hands, looked at it, turned it over. "You'd think if they wanted publicity, their name would be on it somewhere."

He put it back down on his desk and I lunged for it. "Do you have the envelope it came in? Can I see it?"

He was staring at me. "Lilly? Why are you so interested in this obscure little group?"

"I don't know. I think…" I grasped for something, anything. "I thought I saw their picture somewhere." I was getting so good at telling lies, what was one more?

"Great. We can listen to it on the way to our picnic." There was a strange expression on his face.

I asked for the second time, "Do you have the envelope it came in?"

"Somewhere. You want to know their address?" He rooted through his trash until he brought up a padded CD mailer. No return address, but postmarked Boston. "You know this group?"

I shook my head. But I was lying.

I'd never told Greg about the Lilith Java Band. That's one of the little details that I'd kept back, because a casual Google search of "Lilith Java Band" yielded stories of drug abuse, murder—and pornography.

Bridget had already left for lunch with her parents by the time I got to the apartment. It took me a few minutes to stash the CD in the bottom of my sock drawer and change into jeans, boots, a sweater and my raincoat.

Greg picked me up in his VW. He'd bought our sub sandwiches and they were in the backseat in a bag along with bottles of Coke and bags of chips. The subs smelled good and I told him so.

"A twelve-inch meatball sub for me and a six-inch chicken on whole wheat for you."

"Mmm. Just what I wanted." In the twenty minutes or so it took us to get to the ocean, he talked about the band that was doing the music at the conference. He'd seen a YouTube video of them and thought they were great. I listened as the rain continued to create a gray haze through which we drove.

"Sounds great," I said, trying to sound interested. My

thoughts were elsewhere. Mudd had sent that CD to Greg. Mudd had even tried to kill Greg. And I needed to tell him, but I couldn't find the right words.

"You know what would be fun, Lilly? If you could come with me on some of these conferences and play music. You really are that good. Paige and Dave agree with me. Do you have a CD or tape of your songs? I'd love to take it and play it for some of the music people there."

I turned sharply toward him, trying to keep my intake of breath to myself. Why would he ask that? Did he know something, suspect something? I couldn't see his eyes or read his expression. His gaze was fixed at a point on the highway ahead.

I looked down at my hands in my lap, at my fingers with their chipped nail polish. I shook my head and said evenly, "I don't think I'm ready for that." He nodded but said nothing.

While we made our way to the seawall in Boston, it alternately poured and drizzled, but never quite stopped precipitating. As I sat there I wondered why I'd agreed to go on this picnic. Greg and I could never be together because I could never be honest. Spending time together would just be a form of torture. But I couldn't say no.

When we got to the seawall, it was drippy but not pouring. He was able to park fairly close to the rocks. We weren't the only crazy people here in the rain. A child, probably no more than three, clad in a shiny yellow slicker, walked between his parents who held a hand on either side. Beyond them, the sea was as dark as iron.

Greg and I sat in the front seat of his car and watched them. I had a pretty good idea what he was thinking because I was thinking it, too. How had we gotten so far off our path?

And then it started to pour. Not rain, not drips, but the kind of pouring that can soak a person in a minute. It sounded like knives hitting the metal roof. The car almost shook.

He said, "How about we eat our lunch in the car and not venture out?"

"Fine by me."

We both reached into the backseat at the same time and our fingers touched. I looked at him and he looked at me, and neither of us pulled away.

"Lilly," he said. His eyes were so blue I thought I'd cry. "How come we're not talking?"

My gaze on him was steady. "I don't know, Greg." But I did know. We weren't talking because there were things I wouldn't tell him. I pulled my hand away.

We ate our sandwiches and watched rain pour into the sea. I told him that I might be going away for a few days, too.

"Where?" he said.

I looked up, my mouth full of chicken sub. "New Orleans. I need to see an old friend."

He put his Coke into the cup holder. "New Orleans. Isn't that where...?"

"Yes, that's where I lived before I came here. With the man who took advantage of me."

"You've never even told me his name."

"I guess I haven't." I stuffed an errant tomato slice back into my sub. The silence was thick and heavy. He waited for more.

Finally he said, "I wanted to be with you this afternoon because I want to talk. We've spent six months together, and yet there are parts of you that are walled off and are off-limits."

I picked up my sandwich, played with the paper wrapping. I wanted to say, "You're right, Greg," but what came out was, "I could say the same thing about you."

He was quiet for a while. "I suppose you could. But I'm not the one with all the mysterious things happening, with the new e-mail address and the friend I have to see all of the sudden in New Orleans." Greg was getting angry. "You have to talk to me, Lilly, or we have no chance."

I said, "If you knew the real me, you'd go screaming into the night."

"How do you know, Lilly? Try me!"

"You want to know my story? You really want to know everything about me?" I asked quietly.

"I do."

I put my sandwich down. Could I do this? Where would I begin? Should I tell him about the Lilith Java Band? The nights on drugs? The stealing? The alcohol? He was right. He knew very little about me. When I reflect on the past six months, it's mostly me listening to Greg talk about worship styles, music, emergent Christianity, post-modern Christianity, hands-on Christianity. I suddenly realized that this wasn't because Greg was such a talker. It was because I didn't want to tell him anything. Maybe it was time for him to know me, just a little. I opened my mouth and found myself saying, "I feel a kindred sisterhood to the girl who killed your wife."

I think Greg was expecting anything but that. He choked on his Coke and just managed to get the can in the cup holder. His expression was pure shock, but I kept going.

"I feel sorry that she was bounced all over the court system and that her picture was all over the papers. I feel sorry that no one—not one person, not her parents, *no one*—stood beside her. No one showed her any mercy, least of all you. I read what you said in the papers, Greg. I found the articles online. 'She should have the book thrown at her—lock her up for life.' Well, you got your wish, because she *is* locked up. But, Greg, I look at her and I see myself. That girl could have been me."

Throughout the exchange, Greg's expression had slowly gone through a transformation, from shock to rage to grief. He sat in the driver's seat looking straight ahead.

I stopped talking.

"But," he finally stammered, looking up at me with watery eyes. "No one on drugs should drive. No one drinking should get behind a wheel."

"Agreed. But they do. And then people die and they have to live with that for the rest of their lives. And no one changes because people don't care. People just want to throw the book at druggies. No one wants to see the real person behind the drugs and the mistakes."

Tears stung at my eyes. I was finally telling him some of what I'd kept back all these months. "Young girls run away from home and are at the mercy of every sort of

thief who wants to exploit them for whatever awful
purpose they can dream up. It happened to me, Greg—"

I stopped, clamped my mouth shut.

He turned to me. "What do you mean?"

I'd come this far, I might as well keep going, I
thought. "I took drugs, Greg. That's a part of the
sordid story that you don't know. I came here and was
part of a drug-counseling program at the church. It
helped me. I worked hard to change my life, to move
past the drugs and the relationship that was built
around them."

"You told me it was an abusive relationship."

"Would that it was *just* an abusive relationship. I've
done some things I'm not proud of. Lots of things
actually. But I kept all of it hidden because I didn't
want to lose you. I wanted to be a Christian. I tried to
hide my past, but I can't anymore. *Because he's back.*"

I let that statement hang in the air. Greg was staring
ahead at the gray rocks which were being pummeled by
the rain and the waves. The couple with the child were
long gone and we couldn't even see across the bay
anymore.

"Your abusive boyfriend—Michael Binderson."

I looked over at him abruptly. "How do you know his
name?"

"I read the police report about what happened in the
church basement. It's no secret. But you could have told
me first, Lilly."

Greg started the car. I guess our picnic was over. He
kept his eyes looking straight ahead.

"I don't understand why you felt you couldn't trust

me with this right off the bat, right at the beginning. Six months ago, to be precise. Have I ever given you any reason to think that I wouldn't accept your past?"

I was quiet for a moment. "Actually, Greg, yes, you have."

He put the car in gear and we headed out of the lot. We didn't talk on the way home. When we got to my apartment I hesitated and then said, "I'm sorry for what I said back there. About your wife. I had no right."

Greg nodded slightly. He seemed to be waiting for me to get out of the car, so I did. I watched him drive off and then went in. And as I watched him drive away, I knew that nothing had been solved. Nothing had changed.

Bridget was in the apartment when I got there, sorting her knitting yarns by color. She had them lined up on the couch, the darkest to the right side of the couch and the lightest at the other end.

"Oh, hi," she said, looking up. "I didn't think you'd be home for a while, so I've sort of taken over the couch. Sorry. I've got a pot of Irish Cream flavored coffee on if you want some."

"Thanks. That might be nice on a day like today." I pulled off my boots, hung up my jacket and fetched a cup of coffee.

"So? How was your time with Greg?"

I plopped into the rocking chair and held the mug with both hands. "I think it's over, Bridget. I tried to be honest with him, but I said things I never should have said." I felt so heavy, so sad.

Her eyebrows scrunched together. She was sitting

cross-legged on the floor with skeins of various shades of green draped over her shoulders, around her arms, even through her toes. "What happened?"

"I've lost him," I said. "I feel like I'm losing my life, like everything I care about is slowly draining away. I feel hopeless, Bridget. And like no one believes me."

"Lilly, your life isn't hopeless and I believe you. And so does Stuart. He told me."

"He told me that, too." I took a sip of coffee. I couldn't talk about Greg or Mudd or any of that anymore—it was time to change the subject before I melted into a pile of self-pity. "Did you have a nice visit with your parents?"

"I ended up not going. My mom called. She's sick, so I came home."

"But when I got in from church you weren't here."

"I was over at Mrs. Eberline's," she said.

"Is she okay?"

Bridget stopped what she was doing and got a thoughtful look on her face. "It's really weird. Her grandson was there. It seems Mrs. Eberline has gone on a cruise."

"See? And you were doing all that worrying for nothing."

"But she never told me she was going on a cruise, and she would have. You met her—she talks a blue streak, right?"

"Did you ask about the deck?"

She nodded. "He says he's putting in a brand-new deck to surprise her."

"Well, there you go." I pulled a throw over me and drank my coffee while Bridget stood there shifting from foot to foot, a worried crease between her eyes.

TWELVE

That night I got out the CD I'd put in my pocket in Greg's office and looked at the girl. I looked again at the hard set of her jaw, the emptiness in her eyes. Another lifetime, a million miles away from this place. I opened the CD case. There were no liner notes, just that one picture on the front with no identification. The CD was a plain garden-variety recordable CD, nothing else, no inscription anywhere.

The rain fell outside my window, steady and unrelenting as I cocooned myself in my bed with my laptop. I put the CD into my computer, put my earbuds in my ears and waited for it to load.

There were four songs in total. I remembered when we'd recorded them. We had them professionally done. And it had cost a lot, more than we had, much more. Mudd was so sure it was going to propel us right into the big time. It almost did—if I hadn't left, it would have. The demo had won us auditions with several big recording companies.

While the rain poured over everything in Boston, I

listened to an unhappy girl sing her hard, desperate songs about love, about loss, about never quite belonging anywhere.

By the fourth cut, I was crying. I remembered writing it, at a time when I didn't have a clue about how the world worked. The only upbeat song in the bunch, it declared that the world is yours. Anything you want is there for the taking. All you have to do is grab it with both hands and not let go. It didn't matter who you stepped on or over to get it.

With the CD set to repeat. I went to a travel Web site, one that specializes in last-minute fares, and was lucky to find just what I wanted. I'd leave Thursday morning and be home by Saturday night. Then I surfed the Web for information about Michael Binderson and the Lilith Java Band. I was looking for something new, but there was nothing more recent than eight years ago. I'd read all of that many times already. I pulled up a short article about Mudd.

The body of a man, believed to be that of Michael Binderson, has been found dead in a dawn shooting at a bar owned by Mark Pelsar, a known drug dealer. Pelsar is wanted for questioning…

There were articles about various members of the band being arrested on drug-related charges. There was one—and only one—article about the actual music of the Lilith Java Band. Some enterprising young journalist on the entertainment beat had heard us in a club, liked the sound and wanted to talk with me. Mudd intervened and took over the interview, not allowing me or any of the other band members to speak with her directly. There was one picture of me in that paper, looking wild and strung out on drugs. But it wasn't only drugs I was strung out on; it was fear.

I looked up Moira Peterson and found the one picture of her online that I'd seen many times on my Web wanderings. I stared at her face and remembered all the times we'd clung to each other because our friendship was all that we had. We would sit on the couch in the living room of that rundown house, promising that we would stay together always. Blood sisters, we were. And one day we would steal Mudd's money—which was really our money anyway—and when that happened, we would leave together. We'd strike out together and sing. We would not be separated.

The shame of abandoning Moira was almost more than I could bear.

Finally, I turned off the CD and went to sleep.

In the morning, my guitar student, Irma, was waiting for me at the music store for her lesson. She was always early. When I came early, which was most of the time, we began our lesson ahead of schedule. This morning, she sat on the chair outside the practice room, her music books on her lap, her late husband's old Martin in the beat-up case beside her.

"Hello there, Miss Johnson," she said.

"Hi, Irma. How are you?"

"Fine, just fine." She rose with a groan and handed me a small square package of homemade cookies. "Oh, these old knees of mine," she complained. As we entered the piano room, she said, "You just missed your secret admirer."

"What secret admirer?"

"That young man who always hangs around here."

"What young man?"

She huffed and puffed about her knees, opened the case, got out her guitar and sat down on the stool. I took my customary seat beside her and repeated my question as calmly as I could. "What young man, Irma?"

"The young man who always comes in here. Usually when I'm waiting. He's asked me about you on more than one occasion. He's the one who told me a couple of weeks ago about your special day," she said, eyes twinkling.

What was she talking about?

And then I remembered. More than a week ago, after the first e-mailed picture had come in and I'd cancelled with Greg, she'd asked me about my special day.

"That tall chap," she continued. "Wears dark clothes, and that funny hat."

I blinked, fear in the pit of my stomach. "You mean a pork-pie hat?"

"Yes, that's what it's called. I always tell him you're on your way. I have no idea why he doesn't just wait for you. These young people, so busy, always in a hurry."

After Irma's lesson, I asked Rob if he'd seen the guy that Irma had described. He shoved his magnifying headband onto his forehead and shook his head. He'd just come from the workshop where he'd been repairing a guitar since the wee hours. Rob didn't seem to require a lot of sleep and often got to the store at five or six in the morning to work on repairs.

"Nope," he said. "Sorry, doesn't ring any bells."

"Irma says she sees him here all time."

Rob spread his hands wide. "Maybe. I don't know. We do get some strange musician types in here, as you know."

Somehow I got through the rest of the morning and my afternoon music class. If Neil, Tiff or Lora saw anything odd in my demeanor they were too polite to say. After class, I grabbed a coffee and worked on the project for a while before I headed to my car. I saw that someone had put a leaflet under my windshield wiper. I wiped my sweaty palms on the sides of my jeans and pulled it out. Just what I needed, I thought—to be invited to some student political rally when my life is in chaos.

I started to crumple it up to throw it away, and then I saw what it was. It was a flyer for the Lilith Java Band. I gasped, trembling in the sunlight. There was writing along the bottom, advertising a concert on Wednesday, two days away at seven o'clock at the Square Box Theater.

The Square Box is a community theater just off the grounds of the college. It's a boxy building with white clapboard that needs to be painted every other year. It houses a gorgeous grand piano and a small but wonderful one-of-a-kind pipe organ. It's used for student recitals, concerts and the occasional small rock show. I'd been there a number of times.

I looked up from the flyer and noticed that it was under the windshields on other cars, too. Panicked, I ran from car to car, tearing them off. I saw that all the cars in the lot as far as I could see had these flyers on their windshields.

Why is he doing this to me? I knew the answer he would give. He owned me. He owned my voice and I'd run away from a signed contract and lots of money. He'd come to collect what he'd paid for a long time ago. All he'd meant to do in the church basement was to scare me. If he'd wanted me dead, I'd be dead already. He was warning me, setting me up, making me crazy. He didn't want me dead; he wanted me with him, singing again.

I continued to race from car to car, stuffing the flyers into my bag.

"Sorry, wrong date," I said to one student as I tore the flyer from underneath his windshield. I was working in a frenzied rhythm; grab the flyer, reach to my right, shove it into my shoulder bag, then move on to the next car.

"Wrong date," I kept saying to puzzled students. I came upon a chunky, blond guy with tiny gold hoops in both ears and tore the flyer right out of his hand as he was peering down at it.

"Hey!" he said.

"Wrong date, sorry."

"So when's the right date?" he called after me. "They look good."

"Cancelled!" I yelled over my shoulder. "Whole thing's cancelled."

At the far side of the parking lot, I stopped. Every car in the entire lot had a flyer. At this rate, I would be at this all day. Movement suddenly caught my eye. Who was that at the far side of the lot? I shaded my eyes with my hand. His back was to me, but I knew who it was in an instant. I darted to the nearest building and hid behind a pillar, shaking all over.

It was Mudd. He was right there. This time he wasn't just a picture. I should go over there and confront him, I thought—a public parking lot would be a good, safe place to do it. But I couldn't. I just couldn't move.

Over his shoulder he carried a large messenger bag. There was something different about his gait. I looked harder and realized I was wrong. It wasn't Mudd out there.

It was Neil.

I couldn't believe it.

I stayed hidden behind the post and watched him, my mind reeling. I remembered how Neil had come to me this year, in the first class. Why was he so interested in me, so eager to be my friend? Was it because of Mudd? Just what was their connection?

From my vantage point, I watched him—that familiar long-legged stride, the out-of-fashion windbreaker he often wore. I watched as he went from car to car until every last one in the lot had a Lilith Java Band flyer under the windshield. Then he threw the courier bag into his car and drove away.

I stood there a while longer, trying to control myself. I wouldn't let Mudd and Neil get the upper hand—I would remove every flyer. I would take them to my apartment and shove them all into my paper shredder.

On the way home, I thought about Neil and my eyes blurred with angry tears. I was furious that he had betrayed me.

As I drove home with the crushed and crinkled flyers spilling out of my bag and onto the passenger seat, I wondered if Mudd or Neil were watching me even now, following me on the highway. I looked in the rearview mirror but saw nothing out of the ordinary.

As I wended my way through the streets to my apartment, my mind went back to a dozen years ago when I was young and so desperately naive. The only things I had were my songs, my guitar, a bit of piano finesse and my voice. I knew what people said about my voice, how it was deep and bluesy and smoky. That's how that journalist had described it, the one I wasn't allowed to talk to.

I always got the lead in the high-school musicals. It was almost a given, and I loved being on stage. My father faithfully came to my shows; sometimes my mother did, but not often. Even then, I was too smart for my own good. My high-school music teacher encouraged me to go to college and study music. But being the original diva, I knew better than everybody else: I didn't need to study music or take lessons. That was for people who couldn't sing. I already knew how to sing.

After high school, I left home with my guitar on my back and traveled, playing and singing in as many open mikes as I could find. I sang my own songs, stayed in cheap hotels, drank too much and did too many drugs.

And then Mudd found me. He was a drummer, but

also a band manager and concert promoter. He raved about my voice and formed the Lilith Java Band around me before I even knew what was happening. He got a bass player, a lead guitar player and a few back up singers, one of them being Moira.

At first, Mudd took a cut of our profits, but then he demanded more and more, until he was taking it all and giving Moira and me a small allowance. He became obsessive, controlling, demanding, abusive. He wasn't that way with the guys in the band. No, I learned later he was only that way with us.

After he hit me—always in a place where it wouldn't show onstage—he would say, "You and I belong together, Lil." But his love was stifling and possessive. I ended up in the emergency room once, but I was released into his care when he convinced the nurses that I had overdosed and fallen down the stairs. I don't know if they believed him or not, but they let me go. I'm sure the hospital staff was just happy to get rid of a skinny, hollow-eyed druggie.

The house we lived in was a revolving door providing crash space for a steady stream of musicians and groupies. It was a place to bunk for a while, and no one was refused entrance. Moira and I shared the first-floor bedroom. Mudd stayed in the basement, and so did Jason Krane, the bass player. Also in the house were an odd assortment of Mudd's friends and acquaintances, including his younger brother and various relatives. Mudd had names for all of us. Jason was Freak, the lead guitarist was Idiot, Moira was Moron, I was Loser and his little brother, who bunked out on the couch when he got kicked out of a foster home, he called Psychopath.

Sometimes, when Mudd was in a good mood, I would broach the subject of striking out on my own. Whenever I did that, Mudd reminded me that I was his. "I made you who you are, Lilly Johnson. I took you from fifty-dollar bar gigs and turned you into Lilith Java. I made you a star. I knew you were destined for better things, bigger things. You want to be famous, right? No matter what?"

I would nod. Because I did want that. No matter what. I would do anything. Anything. I would put up with his beatings, his control, the way he left me penniless and downtrodden, just for a chance at a top-ten hit and a video on MTV. I even put up with the way he would try to come between Moira and me. If we were sitting on the couch talking, he would come sit between us and change the conversation, trying to pit us against each other. He would put his hands on our legs and tell us how much he loved us both.

When I was finally on that bus by myself heading north, I thought Mudd was dead. So why didn't I go back to Moira knowing that the danger was gone? I've tried to answer that question for the past eight years. Maybe there was a part of me that wanted a brand-new start, away from the drugs, the late nights, the drinking. Maybe there was even a small part of me that wanted to leave Moira.

When I got back home to the apartment, a very excited Bridget met me at the door.

"You," she said, "have a very romantic boyfriend. I think he's apologizing. It's obvious that what you said to him really doesn't matter."

"What do you mean?" I kept my hand over my shoulder bag to keep the flyers from falling out.

"I mean this!" she said, pointing to a rose laid artfully across a card on our coffee table. "It was waiting on the floor outside the door!"

I opened the card, my heart beating faster at the thought of Greg, and read aloud: "I will always love you. I'm looking forward to the concert." No signature. My heart stopped in my chest. Greg hadn't sent this.

"What concert is he talking about?" Bridget said, dancing around me, smiling. "You guys going to a concert?"

I yanked a flyer from my backpack and flattened it on our kitchen table with trembling fingers. "This one," I said. Her eyes widened. "More about my sordid past," I said. "You recognize this girl?"

Bridget picked up the flyer, looked at me, then back down at the flyer. Then at me again, a quizzical expression on her face.

"It's me," I said. "This is the Lilith Java Band. It's the band that almost made me a star, and almost cost me my life. It's the last thing I haven't told you, Bridget."

Throughout the evening, I told her the rest of my story, every bit of it, including the part about Mudd making Moira and me pose nude to make money for our demo. I even told her that part, as hard as it was.

"Lilly, you are a strong and amazing woman. Thank you for sharing your story with me. But it's all in the past now, and you have nothing to be ashamed of," she said gently.

"I'm sorry it took me so long to get my story out. I have so much trouble trusting people."

"I think it's a good thing that you're going to see Moira. I could come with you, if you'd like."

"This is something I need to do on my own. But thanks for the offer," I said.

Bridget gave me a huge hug, told me she loved me. Later, I checked my new e-mail, hoping against hope that Greg would have sent me a message, but my in-box was empty.

Maybe Bridget was right. Maybe going to see Moira was a good thing—it might help me finally lay the past to rest so I could find a future with Greg. That is, if he still wanted a future with me.

THIRTEEN

There was a lot on my plate for the day. I had to be at the music store at eight in the morning to help with inventory. My guitar student Ted was coming in at nine, and then I had a lunch meeting with Neil, Tiff and Lora—I had no idea how I would react to Neil, what I would say to him. After that, I had booked a practice room for an hour, and then I had to pack for New Orleans. Finally, I planned to go to the Square Box for the supposed Lilith Java Band show. Bridget had begged me not to go, but I had to. I had to see who would be there.

I spent the morning helping Rob with inventory. We were incredibly busy and my shift went quickly, which was good—it kept me from checking my phone every few minutes to see if Greg had texted or left a message. I kept wanting to call him, but I knew I should wait for him to call me. I was also waiting for the police to call, but I was pretty sure they wouldn't. They kept insisting Mudd was dead, despite my protests. As far as they were concerned, the case was closed.

At nine-thirty Ted arrived. I had planned to talk with

him about Neil. I looked up from the cash register to see him gazing at me intently. Too intently? Was it really music lessons he wanted, or was he being paid to observe me? I tried to stop myself—where were these paranoid thoughts coming from, anyway?

When Ted came into the room and sat down, I blurted out, "I have to talk to you about Neil. What do you know about him?"

"My neighbor Neil?" His gray pupils loomed large behind his grimy glasses.

"Yes," I said. "I'm just curious to know what you know about him."

"Not much. I don't see him often. I just heard him playing his cello in his room and asked if he knew someone who could teach me the guitar. He's not home a lot."

"He's not home a lot?"

"I think he has a girlfriend." Then he leaned toward me and said conspiratorially, "There's been more than one occasion when he's been away all night."

"Hmm." Was he spending those nights with Mudd? Or could it be Tiff? Had geeky Neil managed to make pretty, pixie Tiff his girlfriend? Who knew the ways of love? I certainly didn't.

After Ted's lesson, Rob bounded in and said to me, "Lilly, you got a telephone message. Dave from your church."

"Thanks."

I called Dave on my cell. Did I have a few minutes today to drop by, he wanted to know. I told him I was up to my ears but I would be back on Saturday.

"This is fairly important," he said, sounding very serious. "Paige is here, too."

I gulped. Okay, then. I guess I'd better go. A part of me feared they'd discovered everything I'd tried to hide and were now going to ask me to leave, rescinding my membership or doing whatever they do to get rid of errant church members. I told Rob I had to leave. "An emergency meeting," I said. I'd make up the time when I got back from New Orleans.

Rob must've seen something in my face because he nodded and said, "Fine, fine. See you Monday. Have a good trip."

When I got to the church, Paige and Dave were waiting for me in Dave's office. I sat down and Dave closed the door, signifying the solemnity of the meeting. I felt a little sick.

I looked from face to face, but neither of them was smiling. Dave opened a folder on his desk, pulling out a copy of the Lilith Java Band flyer, the one advertising the concert. Then he turned it over. Glued to the back was a picture of me from our church Web site. Underneath, in black felt pen, was written one word in large capital letters: RESEMBLANCE?

I was too horrified to even try to explain.

"We're worried about you, Lilly," Dave said.

"Very worried," Paige agreed.

Dave tapped the picture with his finger. "We wanted to talk to you before we call the police. Greg received one of these as well. And Paige. Even Brenda. Greg said he received a CD, too."

I gulped. *Oh God,* I prayed silently, *what do I do?* I

wanted to say, "I was young. I know I made a mistake. I'm so sorry, I should have gone to the police right away when I heard the shot in the bar. But I didn't. And the money? I can explain about the money, too." But the only thing on my mind was, "Where is the CD?"

"Greg has it," Dave said.

I thought about the CD buried underneath my socks. Dave picked up the flyer and studied it. He turned it over. I remained quiet. I just didn't know how or where to begin.

"We think this is serious, Lilly. We think someone, for whatever reason, has fixated on you and that this is part and parcel of what happened to you here in the basement. That whoever is stalking you is sending these pictures as well."

I took a deep breath. It was time I admitted what they already knew. "That girl is me."

Paige was looking at me. She'd known me when I first came here. She had probably recognized me immediately.

"That was my band. It's what I did before I came here. Now, Mudd, er, Michael Binderson from the band, that's him there. He's the one who's stalking me. He was in the basement that night."

"We need to inform the police of this new development," Dave said, putting his reading glasses down on his nose.

"They don't believe me. They keep telling me that Mudd is dead."

Paige leaned forward. "Well, it's time we make them believe he's alive."

"I agree," Dave said.

"I'm leaving tomorrow," I told them. "I've got a plane ticket to visit her." I pointed to Moira, also in the picture—behind me in the shadows, tall and dressed all in black. "She was a friend of mine. She may know where Mudd's been all these years."

"Why don't you just call her?" Paige asked.

"I need to see her," I said. "It's personal."

We talked for a few more minutes and I told them my story. I told them about the abuse, betraying Moira, fleeing to Boston and feeling safe for eight years. I said I suspected that Mudd had found me through the church Web site, and that he probably wanted his money back. I kept my eyes down when I talked.

At the end, I wanted to tell them that I would leave the church, that I wouldn't play music there anymore, but I didn't. I seemed to have run out of words. I just took a deep breath and bowed my head. There were tears on my eyelashes. "Mudd is dangerous."

"We'll take care of that," Dave said. "I'll have a good talk with the police."

I left as quickly as I could after the meeting. I needed air and I needed to get to my meeting with Neil, Tiff and Lora. I made my way down the hallway, but I was aware of steps behind me. I could tell it was Paige, but I just didn't want to talk anymore. I quickened my pace and practically ran down the final hallway. I was about to push the door open when I heard, "Lilly!"

I didn't say anything. I just stood there, my hand on the door. Finally, I mustered my voice. "Yes?" I said.

She looked around as if she didn't want us to talk out in the open. Dave and Brenda were walking toward us, chatting. The flyer was folded up in his hand. The church janitor came in followed by a few construction guys. The church was a regular beehive of activity buzzing around me but all I could do was stand, frozen, in front of the door.

Paige said, "Let me walk you to your car."

"Okay," I said.

We walked a few steps in tandem, then when I beeped my car open with my remote, she said, "That was a brave thing you did in there."

"It didn't feel brave," I admitted. "It felt awful, like I was tearing out my guts."

Paige put a hand on my arm. "It's okay, Lilly," she said.

"You knew it was me from the beginning, didn't you?" I asked.

She nodded. "And I think Greg did, too."

Neil, Tiff and Lora were waiting when I arrived, late by seven minutes. Spread out on the table were pictures, old vinyl records and posters. For one horrifying moment I thought it was Lilith Java Band memorabilia, but it wasn't. I took a quick look at Neil and then decided to shove in beside him. "What's all this?" I asked.

He grinned at me. "Lora got this stuff at the archives. It's all Hungarian folk music."

"Wow," I said without enthusiasm.

Tiff piped up, "We need to listen to these."

"That'll be a joy," Lora said dryly.

I kept my eye on Neil, who seemed no different than all the other times we'd been together. Tall, nerdy plaid shirt, glasses. The same. "Look at this," he said laying down a music score.

I put my hand over it and said, "I have to go to New Orleans tomorrow for a couple of days."

"Really? Cool," Lora said. I carefully watched Neil, but saw nothing. I felt like waving my hand in front of his face and saying, "New Orleans! That ring any bells?" I didn't. He picked up the music score and looked down at it carefully.

Maybe he only knew Mudd from Boston? Well, that was certainly possible. Mudd could have discovered I was here, found out that impressionable Neil was in my class and then recruited him to spy on me.

"Hey," I said to him. "It looks muddy out."

He looked at me, a puzzled expression on his face. "What?"

"Muddy," I said. "Mud. You know, *mud?*"

Still no recognition. He just raised his eyebrows and seemed perplexed. "You think it's muddy out? It hasn't rained in a couple of days. What do you mean?"

"Nothing. Never mind." It was a lame attempt but I didn't know what else to do. I sighed and focused on the stuff on the table. I would need to confront him in private.

My cell phone rang in my bag. I checked it—it was Greg! I excused myself from the table and answered it.

"Greg?"

"Hi, Lilly. I, uh, I'm wondering if you can pick me up at the airport. I've been doing a lot of thinking and I'd like to talk to you."

I'd never been so happy to have to go to the airport in my life.

* * *

I got to Logan Airport at quarter to five only to discover that Greg's plane had been delayed. I'd checked the airline's Web site just prior to leaving, and the delay hadn't been posted. Obviously it had occurred while I drove through Boston traffic to the airport.

I heaved a sigh and sat down on a plastic chair in the waiting area, feeling cold. I zipped up my hoody. I wished I'd brought a book with me but realized I wouldn't be able to concentrate on it—I was too nervous. I checked my watch. I got up and looked at the flight screen. Delayed again. I paced. I bought a coffee I didn't want. Drank half of it. Paced. Threw the rest of the coffee out. Went to the restroom. Combed my hair. The weather was making it extra curly. I wet it a bit so it would fall in nice waves and not frizz out like an overripe dandelion. It had really taken some doing to get this hair of mine to become straight and black.

As I leaned into the mirror and applied lip gloss, I realized that I looked nothing like the girl in the Lilith Java Band posters. If I had completely changed myself on the outside, then why did I feel like the same awkward, scared girl on the inside?

I bought a package of mints and ate them, one after the other. I got up and walked over to the window. I looked at the clock. I looked back at the screen. If the flight was too late, I wouldn't be able to go to the Square Box Theater. And I had to be there. I needed to prove that Mudd was alive.

I watched a pretty but tired looking young mother try to corral four small children who insisted on playing floor hockey in the middle of the wide hallway. I walked over and checked the screen. Delayed yet again. I wandered down the hall and into a gift shop. When I got back the hockey-playing children had spread out crayons and coloring books on the floor and were talking loudly to each other.

At one point I had the crawly feeling that someone was watching me. I couldn't explain it. I'm not one of those people who get those feelings on a regular basis, but I sure had them in the airport. I felt a chill on the back of my neck and pulled my hoody closer, marveling at the children in front of me in short-sleeved T-shirts.

I looked around. Several people were reading newspapers and books. One young man with wide loose pants was bent over a portable DVD player. Nothing out of the ordinary. No trench-coated person covertly peering at me from above a newspaper. No one leaning against a wall pretending to be talking on a cell phone. I wondered if I was really starting to lose my mind.

"If that plane is delayed any longer, I don't know what I'm going to do with these kids."

I looked up. The mother was talking to me as she bounced a restless baby in her lap.

I said, "I'm thinking of my car in the lot. It's going to end up costing me a fortune."

We chatted, which helped pass the time and take my paranoid mind off things. Her husband was in the military and on his way home, finally, from Iraq. I told her how happy I was for her and she grinned and said that he hadn't seen Bethie, the baby, since she was three months old.

I told her I was waiting for my boyfriend. My boyfriend, I called him. I hoped I could rightfully still call him that.

When Greg finally walked through the door, I approached him awkwardly, wishing things were different between us. Could I touch him? Certainly not a kiss, but a touch?

We stood a little apart for a moment. On the other side of the room I could see the mother and four children being swept into an embrace which went on and on. My eyes misted a bit.

And then suddenly, Greg reached out and touched my face with his good hand, leaned forward and kissed me lightly, gently on the lips. When we parted he said, "It's so good to see you again."

"You, too, Greg."

"I missed you."

"Me, too." I felt quivery, unsteady. He took my hand as we made our way through the airport to my car. My thoughts were all over the place, and I had no idea what he was thinking.

He had said he wanted to talk with me; but all the way into town from the airport, normally talkative Greg was silent. I finally said, "So how's your arm?"

"Much better."

"That's good."

A bit of a head nod.

More silence.

"How was the conference?"

"Good. Great." Pause. "Awesome."

"That's good."

More silence.

As I drove, I kept looking at the digital clock on the console. It was already after eight. The concert—or whatever it was that was going to happen at the theater—had started.

As we got closer to where he lived, I said, "Do you mind, Greg, if I stop in at the Square Box Theater for a minute?"

Pensive look. "Sure. That would be okay."

What was going on in his head? We were a few minutes from the Square Box when he finally turned to me and said, "I asked you to pick me up because I wanted to talk to you."

"Okay."

More silence. The night scenery sped by. I waited. Why was everything so hard to talk about these days?

"It's about what you told me the other day. All that stuff about how you felt sorry for the girl who drove that car…"

"I was upset when I said that. I'm really sorry, Greg."

"I know, but what you said…" He shook his head. "I'm not perfect. There's lots of stuff I'm trying to work through."

"I know. Both of us have stuff to work through."

His voice was a monotone when he finally said, "I haven't been totally honest with you either."

I looked sharply at him, veering slightly on the road.

"I know about the concert at the Square Box Theater, and about the Lilith Java Band. I've been doing my own research," he said. "You'd been acting strangely. I didn't know why, and then I got that CD in the mail—" He stopped.

"You listened to it."

He nodded, his eyes straight ahead. "I got it the day you came to the church and told me that you wanted to take me out to dinner. That's why I was a little shaken up that night. When I listened to that CD, I knew it was you." He paused. "And when you practically grabbed it out of my hand, that confirmed everything. But I couldn't figure out why you hadn't told me. So you were in a rock band. Lots of Christian musicians used to be in rock bands. What's the big deal? So I thought there must be something else, something more."

I kept driving, but my fingers gripped the steering wheel more tightly. *I didn't tell you because when I was a part of that band, I did things I wasn't proud of,* I wanted to say. I didn't. I didn't say anything. I just kept driving.

He went on. "I did a bit more research. I read all the articles about the Lilith Java Band. You keep saying that Michael Binderson isn't dead. That's what you told the police."

"He isn't," I retorted.

"I found articles and information about the shooting death of Michael Binderson. A person named Mark Pelsar is in jail now for his murder."

"He's not dead."

"Well, Lilly, I'm beginning to believe you." I almost burst into tears when he said that. "I called the jail—"

"You did what?" I nearly drove off the road.

"I didn't get to talk with Pelsar, but I did get to talk with the warden. It looks to me like the New Orleans police didn't make this particular murder a high priority. The warden said that Mark has always maintained his innocence. He says he was knocked out, and when he awoke, the gun was in his hand. He says he was too fuzzy when he regained consciousness to actually see the body."

I looked at him. "You actually called the jail?" I couldn't believe it. I was so moved by Greg's help that I could barely take in what he was saying.

"I skipped a meeting at the conference and took advantage of the hotel's super-fast Wi-Fi. One report said an unidentified source suggested there was someone else at the scene. I made a bunch of phone calls to reporters who covered the case, but no one's called me back yet."

Greg still didn't know that I'd been there. Had he figured that out, too? It was now or never, I thought.

"I was there," I said. "That 'someone else' was probably me."

He looked at me. "You were there? When he died?"

I told him what happened. He had a concerned look on his face.

"And no one came after you? Not Michael Binderson? Not Mark?"

I said no.

"Didn't you think that was strange?"

"What do you mean?"

"Think of it this way, Lilly. If Mudd had died, wouldn't Mark have come after you? He knew you were in the van."

"I figured Mudd was dead, and Mark didn't care."

"Didn't the police ask you these questions?"

"I never spoke to the police. I was long gone by then."

"And it was after all this that you came here."

"Right."

"And changed who you were."

"And found faith. And you." We were at a red light. "Greg, I'm not the same person I was then."

"I know you're not, Lilly. I guess I was just hurt that you couldn't trust me with your story. I don't want to give up on us. It doesn't matter that you were on drugs a long time ago. It's no big deal."

The light turned green. I pulled ahead. Was there really a chance for us? Greg knew most of my story now, but not all of it. He hadn't seen the worst of the photos. Would he still want to stay after he'd seen them?

I pulled up in front of the Square Box Theater. A light was on. Little, square, white, with a wide staircase in front and long windows flanking the double doors, the place reminded me of a rural church. Just lift the whole thing up and drop it down into a farming community and it would be two services on Sunday and one on Wednesday night, with potlucks in the basement. There was a lone Honda Accord in the parking lot. I pulled in beside it.

We heard the organ, even before we opened the door. Loud and sonorous and deeply beautiful, it reminded me of old church music, the kind you seldom hear anymore.

Inside, the place even looked like a country church with folding wooden chairs facing the front in even rows. The place was empty, except for a white-haired man who was playing the organ down at the front.

The back of his neck was deeply lined and the overhead chandeliers reflected on his pink scalp as he moved in time to the music. He didn't hear us walk down the hardwood floor toward him.

"Hello," I said tentatively as we got closer.

He ignored us and continued playing.

It took him several minutes to finish the piece and he didn't look up until the last loud chord died out. Then he turned, clapped his hands on his knees and looked at us.

"Well now," he said. His voice was musical with an edge of mirth to it.

"I was just wondering—" I said. "Actually, I'm looking for someone. Have you been here a long time?"

"A few hours," he said. "The acoustics in this place are tremendous." He waved his arms around as if music were still in the air.

"Were you here before seven?" Greg asked.

"Came at six-thirty." Then he grinned. "This place has been Grand Central Station tonight—police, youngsters, you name it."

"What do you mean?" Greg asked.

"Well, first there were the young people, many of them dressed in various weird costumes. Then the police came."

"What did the police want?" I asked.

"It was just one officer, but he made sure he talked with everyone. And then me. I think he was looking for drugs. It's usually drugs, isn't it, with these youngsters? Finally, when they left, I went back to my practicing and yet another young man came in, this one stranger than all the rest. He came up and asked me if I'd met *Lil* yet."

Greg looked at me, recognition dawning on his

face. He must have just figured out why I hated being called "Lil."

"What did the guy look like?" I pulled my hair away from my face in a nervous gesture.

"Well now…" He rubbed his chin. "The guy was tall, about yay high." He indicated with his hand. "Short hair, very neat about his person." He ran his pudgy hand across his scalp. "He was slim but not to the point of being too slender. Certainly not hefty like me, and he wore an odd hat."

I felt faint. It was Mudd. I glanced at Greg.

"Did he give you a name? Tell you what he wanted?" Greg asked.

The man shook his head. "He merely asked if I'd seen Lil, and when I said no, that I didn't know who Lil was, he turned on his heel and sat in that backseat back there, listening for a while." The man pointed to a seat on the far left, in the rear of the room. "He was there until just a few minutes ago, actually."

I thanked him and we walked back down the aisle. I was not the least surprised to see a folded Lilith Java Band poster on the seat the man had indicated.

I picked it up and said. "He was here. He was right here." I felt shaky.

"We'll get to the bottom of this, Lilly. I promise," Greg said, taking my hand.

I was so happy Greg was back and on my side now that I hardly knew what to do with myself.

FOURTEEN

Like everyone else who goes to New Orleans, I was unprepared for the devastation after Katrina, even after all these years. A lot of the city still seemed to be a wasteland, and as the cab driver drove me to my hotel, he told me all about where he was when Katrina hit and where he was at the time he heard about it—glued to CNN—and how his family survived. He and his family were the lucky ones, he went on to tell me. Their home wasn't completely destroyed and they were rebuilding. "Some of the neighborhoods are coming back," he said, "but I think a lot won't even try. Lots of people have already relocated. But you know, New Orleans gets in your blood. Even when you leave New Orleans, you can't *leave.*"

I didn't tell him that I'd lived here eight years ago, that I knew its streets, its clubs and bars. I'd sung all over the city. Although at that time everyone talked about what they would do if "the big one" hit—people even wrote songs about it—no one believed it would ever actually happen.

I had chosen to stay at the cheapest hotel I could find within walking distance of where Moira lived. I was given a key for a room on the second floor, by a sleepy woman in a blue tent of a dress. I took the stairs rather than the doubtful-looking elevator.

I'd been in this hotel when I first arrived in New Orleans nine and a half years ago, after Mudd had found me singing in a small club in Mississippi. He said the exposure of New Orleans would be good for my kind of music, which was a bluesy, folk rock with plenty of hard electric undertones. At that time, the small, square room with the faded chenille bedspread, the tiny television and the rusty bathroom fixtures didn't phase me. After sleeping in bus stations, this hotel with its hot water and a bathroom I didn't have to share felt like the lap of luxury.

I sat down on the saggy bed now and wondered if I were truly crazy in coming here on the spur of the moment. What if I couldn't find Moira? What if I could find her, but she wouldn't talk to me? Why hadn't I at least called first? Why hadn't I? How stupid was that? I was counting on the element of surprise. If I'd called ahead, she would have too much time to prepare for me—to think things through, to refuse to talk, to flee—and I needed to see her.

I unpacked the few things I'd thrown into my carry-on and set off walking the six blocks to the house. There was no reason to put it off. It was very warm here and no autumn colors dotted the landscape. Fall in New Orleans is not fall in Boston. Yet New Orleans has a beauty, and even with the changes after Katrina, it held onto its unmistakable charm. Vines grew over wrought-iron gates and big-leafed flowers in vibrant colors lined the sidewalk. It was more than warm—it was hot, and I quickly tore off the jacket I'd brought with me.

I walked past an elderly gentleman with two small dogs on leashes. When they came over and sniffed at my ankles, I bent down to pet them, welcoming the opportunity to postpone my arrival at Moira's, even for a second or two. "Such cute things," I told him. He wished me good day. He had no idea how much I needed a good day.

I found the little house with no trouble, none at all, and I stood on the street and looked at it for a long time. It was smaller than I remembered, an ugly flamingo-pink box, faded now, the aged boards cracking in places. There was one large window to the left of the door which looked like it was covered inside with a large sheet in a gaudy floral design. On the other side of the door, which stood open, was a small window with shutters a darker pink than the rest of the house. The curtains were drawn.

I knew what lay behind those curtains: a small room with dirty yellow walls. It was where Moira and I slept on two single beds, when I wasn't downstairs in Mudd's room with him. Mudd slept on a sleeping bag in the basement next to the room he used as a studio. I hated it down there. Dark and dank, it always smelled.

I remembered with a shudder the time Moira and I decided to put a lock on our door. Band members and groupies busted in at all hours of the day and night. We'd gone out and bought a cheap little pull-chain lock, which Mudd easily broke. He shoved us around and screamed at us for even thinking about locking the door.

I wondered idly what Moira had done with my stuff. When I'd simply walked away, I had not looked back. I didn't care about my clothes—I was happy to leave behind the leather I wore onstage—but I did miss my guitar. It had been an unexpected gift from my father when I decided to go on the road after high school.

I thought I saw a vague movement at the window. I watched, feeling chilled despite the afternoon heat. The bedroom, I knew, opened onto a living room with that picture window. We had no furniture in those days, except for a ratty couch with tufts of stuffing coming out. It was an awful thing that I was sure was home to families of mice. But we never paid much attention to it, since we all mostly sat around on the linoleum floor anyway.

Down a short hall, was another bedroom reserved for whatever lead guitarists Mudd had lined up. A lot of people came and went in the Lilith Java Band. We could always count on a few sleeping bags thrown hastily on the living room or the kitchen floor.

Opposite a bedroom was a filthy bathroom. At the back of the house was the kitchen, another grime and insect-filled place. We seldom cooked our own food. The only one who did was Jason, the bass player, who for some reason I always trusted. He seemed to be a decent guy, one of the few in the band. While the rest of us just bought takeout when we felt like eating, Jason often cooked Cajun food and regaled us with how many cockroaches he'd killed in the kitchen while cooking.

The neighbors, of course, complained often and

heartily, calling the place a crack house. But Mudd seemed to know in advance when the cops would come, and the house would be clean—dishes washed and floor mopped—and no drugs in evidence when they pulled up, lights flashing.

I glanced at the other houses as I stood here. I hadn't paid much attention to our neighbors at the time. Now I saw an elderly woman with thick ankles in a cotton dress and flip-flops watering a window flower box with a green plastic watering can. Someone on the other side of the house was mowing a lawn. This was a street of poor working people trying to make the best of what life had dealt them. All of the houses were small; most were fairly tidy.

As I stood gazing at this place that held so many memories for me, I began to notice details. Even though the paint was chipped and flaked, the lawn was neat and flowers lined the flagstone path to the front door. I didn't recall the flagstones. I remembered uneven, broken cement squares.

I could put my task off no longer. I walked slowly up the path and then stood on the porch. There were children's toys there; a miniature baby stroller with a blanket-covered doll stood just outside the door.

From around the back of the house came a little girl of about eight or so who wore bright red shorts and a T-shirt with a huge sunflower on it. She stopped in her tracks when she saw me.

"Who are you?" Her hair was brown and thick, tied up in two messy ponytails. She looked like Moira, exactly like Moira.

"Hi." I bent down. "I'm looking for your mommy." She turned and raced inside, the screen door slamming loudly. A few minutes later, a tired-looking Moira in frayed short denim shorts and a tank top was standing in front of me.

"Yes?" she said.

I was looking into the face of my former best friend. I couldn't speak.

The little girl asked, "Can I go to Kim's? Mommy? Is that okay, Mommy?"

Moira stared at me and she didn't answer her daughter.

"Mom-eee?"

"Go. But be home before dark." Her voice was flat and her eyes never left me.

I watched the little girl trot off, her back straight and proud like her mother's. A few moments later Moira said, "Lil?"

"Yes," I said moving toward her. "It's me. I go by Lilly now."

She frowned and backed away into her house, closed the screen door and stood behind it. A look of disbelief or anger—I couldn't tell which—spread across her face.

"You're dead. Everybody thinks you're dead," she said.

"I'm not dead."

Through the screen door her face looked mottled and spotted.

"Your hair. You're a ghost."

"I'm not dead, Moira. And neither is Mudd."

"Where is he? Is he with you?"

"He's been stalking me. I live in Boston now, and he's found me after all these years. I came down here because I...I wanted to see you." I was stumbling over my words. Why *had* I come? To make amends, I reminded myself. To move on.

"You've been alive all this time?" She opened the door a crack.

"I'm..." I paused. "Moira, I'm sorry. That's why I've come back. To tell you how sorry I am."

"Sorry for what?"

"For leaving. For not coming back. For not telling you where I was."

She opened the door the rest of the way, staring. "You look so different. *Your hair.*"

I fingered it. "I know. It's red. Or reddish, I guess. And I haven't straightened it in a long time. This is how it is in real life, curly."

"Have you seen Mudd?"

"No, but other people have."

She kept looking at me. I used to think that Moira was just about the most beautiful woman I'd ever seen. With her dark eyes, classic cheekbones and full lips she had a model's good looks. But now, faint lines were drawn around her eyes and her cheeks looked slightly gaunt. You could see the bones of her face too clearly.

I continued, "When I left, I had no idea he was still alive. I never would have left you with him. It must have been horrible for you. For everyone."

She cocked her head and stared at me. "What are you

talking about? I haven't seen Mudd since the morning he died. Mark, that guy from the bar, killed him."

"There's something funny about that, though. Mark has always said he didn't do it."

"We all thought that you killed him."

"What?"

"We thought maybe you had just had enough one day, killed him yourself and ran off. So none of us told the police anything about you. We thought you'd be back. We waited and waited for you, but when you didn't come we thought you were dead, too. Because you *would* have come back if you were alive."

"I'm here now," I said.

"A little late, don't you think?"

We were both quiet after that. Perhaps she, too, was remembering the time we made a promise to each other. It was after a gig. We had done well, or at least we thought we had. We'd played the new song I'd written about grabbing for life with both hands. Besides what we were paid, we always laid our guitar case open in front of us. On a good night it would be filled with fives, tens, even twenties. Moira and I got to it before Mudd did. It was our money after all. One night, we were in the process of divvying it up when Mudd came and took it. After that, I decided that we needed to strike out on our own. But Moira wanted to wait. Mudd was close to signing a record deal. Mudd held the keys and he was smart and a savvy businessman and without his backing we'd be back to doing bar gigs with only an open guitar case. We decided then that the only way to survive Mudd was to stick together—always. Where one went the other would go. And one day, we would find a way to get our money back; we'd steal it if we had to, and when we did so, we'd run, the two of us together. Always together.

And then I had taken Mudd's money and run away by myself.

I looked back to the woman on the other side of the threshold. "But how could you not come? No phone call? Nothing to let us know you were okay?" she said.

I felt my eyes well up. "I'm so sorry, Moira. I was afraid. I was just afraid. There's no excuse. I know that." Then Moira did something surprising. She came to me, and put her arms around me. We embraced each other for a long time. Her thin shoulders heaved. When we pulled apart, she said, "You need to come in, get out of the heat. I have some iced tea."

I followed her inside. The rotten, mouse infested couch had been replaced with a navy blue sofa with a couple of gold throw cushions with tassels. It didn't look new, but it was clean. It was flanked on either side by white wicker chairs. The grungy linoleum was covered with wall-to-wall beige carpeting.

There was a TV in the corner, a wooden coffee table, a couple of end tables, a fashion magazine, some unlit candles. Everything was spotless. The place smelled nice, too, as if it had been recently scrubbed down with lemon cleanser. It looked cared for.

"I can't believe you live here," I said.

"I know, but Jason and I have changed it all. We're married now."

I stopped, stared at her. "Jason? You and Jason?"

Moira nodded, smiling.

"Good for you. And you have a little girl. She's pretty. She looks like you."

Her face darkened and she drew away from me, heading down the hall toward the kitchen. I followed her. The kitchen had been completely renovated and looked fresh and clean with new cabinets and cupboards. But the chair I sat on, and the table I sat behind, were the same grimy metal table and chairs that we had used. No matter how hard we'd scrubbed, they'd still look grungy.

She opened up the fridge, pulled out a plastic pitcher of iced tea and poured two glasses.

"Maggie is Mudd's child," she said simply.

I gaped at her, my hands on the table.

"I was pregnant when you disappeared," she continued. "He raped me. Plain and simple." She pulled out a packet of cigarettes and shook one out. "My one bad habit from the old days. I've tried a million times to quit. Can't. So I just give in, even though it's all but ruined my voice." She put the cigarette to her mouth and lit it. "Just before he died, that's when it happened. But Mudd was always obsessed with *you*, Lil. Always. After he died, Jason and I went through his things, and found picture after picture of you. Hundreds of them."

I thought about all the pictures that had been e-mailed to me. Maybe his obsession had grown through the years to the point of madness. "What happened to the pictures? What did you do with them?"

"His mother came and got all his things."

"I remember her. The drunk. Wasn't she the one who owned this house to begin with?"

Moira nodded. "It was in her name. After Mudd died she put the house up for sale, and Jason bought it for a song. It was a mess. We're still working on it."

"Was it damaged in Katrina?"

She took a long drag on her cigarette and placed it on the edge of her ashtray as she exhaled. "Oh, Lil, that was such a horrible, horrible time. I still have nightmares about it. Maggie was only five. We got out, the three of us, but the highways were packed. We landed with an aunt of Jason's in Mississippi. You remember Carly and Joe? That restaurant we used to sing at sometimes? They refused to evacuate—a lot of die-hards did—and their restaurant was totally destroyed and no one ever found them."

"You were lucky then."

"No one in New Orleans feels very lucky. We were all hurt. The house had some damage, but it was salvageable. We had water in the basement up to the main floor." She tapped the kitchen floor with her sandaled foot. "But we weren't flooded to the rooftops like they were in the Ninth Ward." She took another drag. "It's a different city now."

"It seems so."

I took a sip of my tea. It was wonderfully cold and flavored with freshly picked mint leaves.

She ran a hand through her beautiful wayward hair, picked it all up, held it off her neck for a few seconds and then let it drop.

"Do you still sing?" I asked.

She shook her head. "Not so much anymore. Things are all different now. Just mostly the tourist places are open. What about you? You were the one with the voice. I hope you don't smoke."

I shook my head. Even in the old days of my craziness, I avoided inhaling anything, knowing it would destroy my voice.

I looked out of the back window into a fenced backyard with a children's bicycle, a swing set and a small round pool half filled with water.

"Does Jason still play? He was so good on the bass."

She shook her head. "He works in the French Quarter. He drives a horse and buggy for the tourists."

I opened my eyes wide and smiled. "You're kidding me!"

"I kid you not. And he loves it, actually. It suits him. You know how he is with people. It's not a great living, but we get by. I work as a waitress part-time."

We chatted on for a few more minutes until we ran out of small talk. The silence lengthened. Finally she said, "You need to tell me. What happened on that day you left?"

I leaned back in my chair and told her that eight years ago I was sleeping off a long night when Mudd came into my room early and shook me out of bed. He'd said we were meeting with some music-industry professionals, so I finally roused myself, threw on a pair of jeans and a T-shirt and went with him.

"I remember that," Moira said. "I remember him coming in and waking you up that morning. You shoved him and said, 'Go away.'"

I nodded.

"That's the last time I saw either of you," she said.

"I didn't really believe we had a meeting. I had no idea why Mudd wanted me up so early. But it was getting so that Mudd wouldn't let me out of his sight and he would demand that I go along with him everywhere."

"I told you. He was obsessed with you."

And still is, I thought with a shudder. A slight breeze wafted through the open kitchen window. It felt good. I collected my thoughts. It was a story I'd gone over so many times, but now that I was talking about the particulars with Moira for the first time, I was having trouble working the phrases into sentences.

"We ended up taking the van," I said, "which I thought was kind of strange. We only used the van when we were hauling gear. But I climbed into the front seat—Mudd had never offered any explanations for anything he did, so I just went along. All I had with me was my wallet with hardly any money in it. The whole way there Mudd is like, 'Lil, you remember something. I own you. I own your voice and don't you forget it.' He'd told me that a hundred times and I was starting to believe him. And then we got to Mark's."

Moira said, "What a sleaze. I never trusted him. I hated when we played at his bar. He always used to leer at me."

"Yeah, he was gross, but he was our main supply of drugs. Anyway, Mudd says to me, 'I have to make a stop before the meeting.' I'm thinking, 'Oh great. I have to be here when Mudd gets his weekly supply of drugs. Not how I want to start my day.' I told him I'd just wait in the van, and he grabbed my chin and said he needed me to come in. As a witness, he said. He had his backpack with him, and it was full.

"As we go in, Mudd is holding on to my shoulder. We go into the back room and Mark is there, sitting behind a table. On a table is a small suitcase with all these little bags of white powder. He and Mudd start talking, and then they start arguing. I mean really arguing. And suddenly I'm afraid. Mudd is still holding on to his backpack. Mark takes out a gun and aims it at Mudd. By this time, I'm in the doorway. I do not want to get in the way of any gunfire.

"Suddenly Mudd throws me his backpack and says, 'In the van! Go!' And while I'm running to the van I hear a shot. I climb inside and wait for a minute. I'm shaking. I'm shivering. I get out of the van. I start to go back into Mark's but I don't. I'm afraid of what I might see. And then I realize something. Someone got killed here. And I was a witness. If Mudd died, Mark will come after me. And if Mark died, Mudd will think I saw something and realize I had to run."

The events of that morning came back to me with crystal clarity as I continued on with the story. "The backpack was heavy and when Mudd threw it in my direction he figured I would take it to the van without opening it to look at its contents. That he could trust me with it was proof of just how much control he held over me.

"I ended up at the bus station and bought a ticket for Nashville. I thought maybe I could go there and sing. But when I got to Nashville, I knew I needed to go farther. I bought a ticket for New York. But even New

York didn't feel far enough away. I only had enough money to go to Boston, so that's where I went. I still had not looked inside the backpack. I was sure the thing was full of drugs. In the cubicle bathroom in the Grey-hound station I opened it for the first time, intending to flush the drugs down the toilet. The backpack was entirely filled with fifty and hundred dollar bills. This was our money, mine and yours, the money we had dreamed about, planned to get our start with."

Moira was listening carefully. I couldn't tell what she was thinking.

"In Boston, I checked into a motel and paid for it with cash from the backpack. I hid there for a week, sure that Mudd was going to come for his money. But then he didn't. I found an apartment and rented it with cash."

"What did you do with the rest of the money?" Moira asked me now.

I looked into my iced tea. "I spent it all. Every penny. I got myself a nice apartment. I got a job in a music store. I bought a new guitar. And when it was gone, I started going to church."

"Church!" She lit another cigarette, having long since finished her first one.

She took a long drag and didn't say anything for quite a while. Then, "You could have saved yourself a lot of grief. Mudd is dead."

"Did you actually see his body?

"No, but the news said it was Mudd."

"He didn't die that day, Moira. He saw an opportu-nity and went into hiding. But I bet he was looking for me the whole time, incensed that I took his money. I'm sure he was hoping to find Lilly Johnson in the same place he found me the first time, in clubs and at open mikes. He was looking for me in all the wrong places. A few months ago, though, my picture was posted on my church's Web site, and Mudd found it. I don't know, maybe he Googles 'Lilith Java Band' or my name once a month. He's been stalking me ever since."

Moira looked out the window, not saying a word.

"Another reason I came, Moira, was to make it right about the money. There was sixty thousand dollars in that backpack, and so I owe you thirty thousand. I want to begin paying you back, to prove how sorry I am. I want to repay you the thirty thousand dollars."

Moira looked at me intently. She did not smile. Finally she stubbed out her cigarette in the ashtray and squinted her eyes at me.

"I don't want your money, Lil. Don't insult me by asking again. I thought we were better friends than that."

I put my hands around my glass of iced tea and gazed into its depths. "Moira, I wish I knew what to say to make it all right. I was young and stupid. I have no excuse."

"I'm sure Mudd is dead. He's never been back. And he *would* have come, at least to get his stuff. But if you want to, we could go and talk to Jason. He was the one who talked to the cops eight years ago. He was there when Mudd's mother came for his stuff. Let me give him a call on his cell. I'll also see if Maggie can stay with Kim for a couple more hours." She picked up her phone, then turned back to me. "I don't care about the money, Lilly. I never did. I just wanted to know what happened to *you*. That's all I cared about."

FIFTEEN

As we drove to the French Quarter, she, like the cab driver, pointed out all the changes in the city.

"So many things are different now," she said as we made our way down the once familiar streets. I didn't know whether she was referring to her life or the city. Perhaps both. Traveling the terrain was strange, like driving through a dream. In many ways, the city looked no different. But in other ways, it was vastly changed. A lot of the old trees were no longer there, replaced by leafy green foliage that had grown up quickly to take their place.

It was hot in the car, and Moira cranked up the AC. The cool blast felt good on my face. As we got closer to the French Quarter, she told me about the day Mudd and I disappeared. She remembered the early morning when Mudd came into the room and woke me up.

"I thought, *now what,* but immediately went back to sleep. I woke up a little after noon and wandered into the kitchen to see if there was anything to eat. Heather—do you remember Heather?"

I nodded. "That lead guitar player's girlfriend. But I can't remember his name."

"Heather's in there making coffee and I ask if she's seen you or Mudd. She shakes her head. I spend the day watching television and waiting. Mudd's stupid little brother shows up then. You remember him? He's looking for Mudd. Various other people show up during the day looking for Mudd and you. I was in a kind of a daze that day. Before I know it, it's late at night. I begin to worry. So does Jason. Jason calls the police. But they don't take our call seriously. I guess we weren't their favorite people. Then, we turn on the TV, and we hear about Mudd's death. The police came the next day."

"Alleged death," I corrected her.

"The cops came around a couple of times. We thought you'd killed Mudd, since Mark was denying it, so we never told them about you, that you'd gone with him. We just waited for you to come home."

I had nothing to say to that.

"And then Mudd's mother shows up. Boy, that was an experience!" She shook her head.

"How so?" I asked.

"She comes in a cab and I swear she's drunk out of her mind." Moira gestured wildly as she talked. "She's hollering and yelling about how we killed her son, and finally Jason just gets all of Mudd's stuff, puts it in a box and throws it on the front porch. She takes off then."

"Did that include my clothing? My guitar?"

She nodded. "By that time, we thought you were either dead or in temporary hiding." There was the slightest emphasis on the word temporary. "It was Jason's idea to get rid of your stuff, so if the police came sniffing around again there would be no record of you. We didn't want to throw it out, though. Then when she showed up, we just gave the stuff to her."

I nodded.

"You'll see the French Quarter isn't much changed," she said. "The city got it fixed up first, you know, for the tourists."

She parked on a side street and we walked. It gave me a strange sort of déjà vu to wander down the streets with their antiques and jewelry stores, pawnshops and strange voodoo shops. When we got to the street where the carriages lined up to wait for tourists, I recognized Jason immediately—his big, clumsy teddy-bear body leaning against his buggy, and that perpetual grin of his. I used to wonder how his big fingers could manage all those bass guitar licks, but they did. He was an expert.

His eyes grew into saucers when he saw me and his smile widened even more, if that were possible. "I couldn't believe it when Moira called. You're here. And you're not dead."

I went to him. "The rumors of my death have been highly exaggerated. Yes, it's really me."

He gave me a bear hug. "Your hair," he said.

"That's exactly what Moira said to me—'your hair.'" I touched it. "It isn't black anymore. Or straight."

"I like it."

"Thanks."

"We all should get coffee someplace." He turned to Moira. "And something to eat. Isn't it time for a meal yet?"

She linked her arm in his and said, "Oh, you're always hungry."

He made sure his horse Prince, was securely tied, and we chose a coffee shop where he could keep an eye on the buggy. Over plates of dirty rice and jambalaya, we chatted about old times. Jason filled me in on all the old band members and all the old haunts. I told him all about Mudd and how he was in Boston now and how I was sure he wanted his money. We ended with cappuccinos while Jason tried to convince me that Mudd was dead.

"They found his body. They found his wallet. And Mark is in prison for his murder."

I shook my head. "I know I'm right in this, Jason. Who taped the picture of him up in the church basement if it wasn't Mudd?"

"Lil could be right," Moira said. "I always thought there was something strange about the whole thing. I don't think the police really looked into it carefully. You agreed with me at the time, remember?"

"See?" I said to him. "She's right."

He put down his cappuccino.

"Maybe," he said. "But it's a stretch. I know Mudd and he would've come back to the house."

Moira lit another cigarette and Jason grabbed it from her hand. "I thought you were trying to quit."

"Oh, Jason, I'm trying." She leaned over and gave him a kiss. I suddenly missed Greg and felt a pang of guilt about the things he still didn't know. We weren't exactly broken up, but we weren't together, either. It was so confusing.

They persuaded me to check out of my hotel and stay with them, saying they'd drive me to the airport in the morning. When I told them about my music, they asked to hear a song. So I sang one of my own worship songs for them, a little nervous about how they'd react.

Jason grinned, lighting up his big, round face. "You still have your beautiful voice. That hasn't changed."

Moira added, "And you have that ability to string words into beautiful songs."

The four of us, including Maggie, spent the evening singing and playing. Maggie, who'd seemed shy when I arrived, opened right up and sang. She had a beautiful voice and I told her that she sounded just like her mother. Both of them grinned at me.

After Maggie went to bed, Jason asked me how I ended up in a church.

I told them that the church had a drug-counseling program in the basement three nights a week, which was good. I got myself back on track but I really had no intention of ever going to a Sunday morning service. I had no need for God.

I don't know really what made me go into that church the first time. I told them on Sunday mornings I would look out my window and see the steeple and the cross. Just seeing them gave me an odd sort of comfort. I couldn't explain it. There was such an emptiness in me, a loneliness. I desperately wanted to call Moira, but I didn't dare. I'd taken the money we'd promised to share and I was going through it like water.

Then, one Sunday morning, I walked to church and sat in the back row in the chair closest to the door. I left before anyone could talk to me. That became my pattern for many months. I wanted something, someone to take away my loneliness and fear. My hair was still black then, and I wore it long so I could bend my head down and hide my face. I had no Bible and could barely follow the service, but still I went, week after week, and sat in the same place.

It was the music that reached me first, music so hopeful and joyous. I wanted whatever God was being praised and worshipped in the cadences of those hymns. Gradually, I began to lift my eyes, and as I continued to go, the songs, some of them at least, became familiar to me.

I began to sing again.

Also, by this time, the black was growing out of my hair. I had it cut very short and it curled. I doubt that there were too many people in the rather large church who would even remember that I was that girl with the black hair and piercings.

The second thing that changed me was the people. Even when I wouldn't talk to any of them, they talked to me, and seemed to accept me for who I was. Paige came to me and said she'd heard me sing and that I had an extraordinary voice. It was Paige who got me involved in church music.

When Greg came on the staff a few years later and we fell in love, I began to believe that I could have it all: a wonderful husband and a life of serving God. I believed that, just as the Bible says, the old is passed away. But I kept most of my past life a secret from Greg and everyone else. And then, I told them, a little over a week ago everything began to unravel.

"Do the police believe that Mudd is alive?" Jason asked.

I shook my head, and told them what Greg had found out. Just mentioning his name gave me a pang. I wished he were here to meet these friends of mine.

"The police are convinced that Mudd is dead," I said, "but I'm just as convinced that he's alive."

"You need to go on home and make them believe that all of the things that have happened to you are not unrelated," Jason said.

I didn't know if I could, but I owed it to myself— and to Greg—to try.

It was difficult saying goodbye to them the following morning at the airport, but I promised to keep in touch. Moira hugged me tightly and Jason kissed me lightly on both cheeks. I hoped I would have the chance to see them again.

The first part of my flight was quick. The plane left on time and I arrived in Houston right on schedule. I had an hour layover before the flight left for Boston. I bought a magazine and sat down to read, but couldn't concentrate. Instead, I thought about Jason and Moira and Maggie. They always say "better late than never," but sometimes I think a person *can* be too late with some things. I knew that if Mudd hadn't come back, hadn't started stalking me, I never would have made this trip back. I never would have admitted all that I had to Greg. I would have gone on pretending that the past hadn't existed. I would have saved myself a lot of trouble if I had just been honest from the start.

I closed the magazine and checked my voice messages. There were two; the first was from Bridget and the second from Neil, of all people. But none from Greg. I chided myself for continuing to hope.

Bridget said, "Hey Lilly, how're you doing? I hope things are going well for you in New Orleans. I've got your arrival time and I'll be there in plenty of time to pick you up. I'm just on my way over to Mrs. Eberline's. I'm worried about her. I just didn't believe her grandson when he said she went on a cruise. So, I've decided to go talk to him again. Maybe I'm just being paranoid, but I can't get her out of my mind. Anyway," her voice brightened, "I'll see you soon."

I called Bridget and got her voice mail.

The second message was from Neil, asking if I could meet with Tiff, Lora and him on Sunday afternoon. "I know it's not our usual time, but we were wondering if you could come then," he said on the message.

I pressed his number into my cell and decided that this was my chance. It was time he told me the truth.

"Hey, Lilly, you get my message?"

"Neil." I kept my voice even. "You have to tell me how you know Mudd. This is serious now. Things have happened."

"How do I know what?"

"Mudd."

There was a pause. "You mean like dirt? What are you talking about?"

My head was beginning to hurt. The voice on the PA system was loudly calling flights. An older couple in big flowered shirts, laden with straw bags, sat within earshot of me. I moved away, found another corner. I said, "I want to know your connection with Michael Binderson, also known as Mudd." I lowered my voice, trying to keep the rising panic from breaking out all over me. The last thing I needed was airport security after me. "I know you're connected to him, Neil. Did he send you to Boston to spy on me? Is that why we're so conveniently in the same study group?" I felt cold and hugged my arms around me.

Now his voice rose. "Is this a joke, Lilly? I've never heard you like this."

"I saw you, Neil, last week, putting flyers on the cars in the parking lot."

"What cars? Lilly, you've been acting strange now for a couple of weeks, but this is ridiculous. Wait—you mean those flyers about that girl band?"

I closed my eyes and leaned into the wall. I was so full of pent-up energy I thought I would explode.

"Yes," I said with as much calm as I could muster. "That girl band."

"That was just some guy in the student union building who asked me if I wouldn't mind doing that for him. He said he'd buy me a coffee. He seemed in a hurry. So he did one side and I did the other," he said. "And I thought, here he is advertising a band, like, two days before the event, well, I'd be nervous, too. But when I went to give him his bag and get my coffee, he was gone."

I willed myself to remain composed. All this time I'd been blaming geeky Neil for things he knew nothing about. "Neil, can you describe this guy to me?"

"I guess the most distinguishing feature was a funky hat he wore."

My heart fell. What more proof did I need?

"What did you do with the bag, Neil?"

"I kept it. I couldn't find the guy so I took it with me."

"And you have it now?" My voice rose dangerously at the end. A man looked over at me curiously. I willed myself to lower my voice.

"I have it now."

"Could you look and see if there's any address or anything on it? If you find anything, or remember anything—anything he may have told you—could you get back to me right away?"

"Sure. No problem."

I hung up, and then tried Bridget's phone again. I felt a vague unease I couldn't explain when she didn't answer for the second time.

SIXTEEN

We were a long time on the tarmac, awaiting clearance. All that time I could do nothing but sit crunched into the window seat, wishing we were in the air. My fear continued to rise. Mudd was alive. Irma had seen him. The organist had seen him. And now Neil. And why wasn't Bridget answering her cell?

The only thing that gave me comfort was the fact that I didn't think Mudd wanted to kill me. If he'd wanted to do that, he would have done it already—in the church basement, in my apartment, at school. So what did he want? Was it about the money?

My breath was coming out in gasps as I looked out of the window. My cell phone vibrated in my jacket pocket and when I saw it was from Neil, I turned my face to the window and quietly answered it. I was sure this wasn't allowed—talking on a cell phone prior to take off—but I had to talk with him.

"Neil?" I said.

"Lilly, I found that bag that you were talking about. There was an envelope at the bottom. It may be nothing because it was addressed to 'Occupant,' but you said to call if I found anything, so I thought you'd want to know this. Are you on the plane yet?"

"Yeah," I said as quietly as I could, "we'll be taking off soon."

"There was a street address on it."

"Miss?" Out of the corner of my eye, I could see a flight attendant leaning over the two people next to me, trying to get my attention. I faced the window and pretended I didn't see her. "Miss? You'll have to turn off your cell phone. We'll be taking off soon."

"Neil," I said, "quickly, what is the address?"

He read it and I memorized it.

"Miss?" the persistent flight attendant said firmly. "You'll have to turn off your cell phone. Now."

I clamped my phone shut, looked up at her, managed a smile and said, "Sorry. I thought that was only when we were flying."

She frowned a bit and hurried down the aisle.

I grabbed a pen from my bag and wrote the address on my hand before I forgot it. As I wrote it down I realized with a horrid, sinking feeling that the address was the residence directly behind my apartment.

No. It couldn't be. I grabbed my PDA from my bag and checked. Yes, there was no doubt. Could this be Mrs. Eberline's apartment? What did it mean? And then I groaned. I realized why I had felt that strange unease. What had Bridget told me? A man claiming to be Mrs. Eberline's grandson said that she was on a cruise. I thought back over the week, remembering the changes in the backyard behind us. As realization dawned, I placed my right palm against the coolness of the window. I knew what had happened. Mudd was the so-called "grandson" who'd told Bridget Mrs. Eberline was on a cruise. But what had happened in the garden?

Our plane was backing out onto the runway. While our flight attendant was snapping the oxygen mask and instructing us to put our own masks on first should the need arise, my fingers were gripping the glass, like I was trying to claw my way out of the plane. I pictured the pile of dirt in her backyard and realized with a rising horror that Mudd could have killed Mrs. Eberline and buried her in the garden. And Bridget was at Mrs. Eberline's right now!

My fingers trembled on the glass and I felt heat rise within me. I wanted to stand up in the middle of the plane and scream, *"My ex-boyfriend killed my neighbor and buried her in the garden! Please! We need to call the police! Now!"*

But I knew what they did with people who caused commotions of any kind on airplanes. They escorted them off in handcuffs and it made CNN. No, my best bet would be to remain quiet.

Breathe deep. Remain calm. *God,* I silently prayed. *Please watch over Bridget.*

Maybe Bridget hadn't gone over there. *Please, God, please make her not have gone there.* Maybe she'd contacted the landlord. I thought about all the times Bridget and I had stood at the kitchen window looking out onto the yard between the apartments. We didn't even have curtains. Mudd could easily have been spying on me. How clever of him to have chosen that apartment. He'd sure done his homework.

I felt sick to my stomach and had to clutch my middle and lean forward. Hopefully those around me would merely assume I was a nervous flyer. I grabbed the sick bag from the seat compartment just in case.

We were speeding down the runway now. I leaned back and rested my head against the back of the chair, trying not to shiver. *Please, God.* Every breath was a prayer. It got so that I didn't even know that I was praying anymore. I was just muttering, *God, God, God,* as we finally—finally—became airborne.

When we were cruising toward home at thirty-seven thousand feet, I closed my eyes but knew that I wouldn't sleep. I kept seeing images of Mudd beating Bridget the way he beat me. Shoving, pushing, belittling... *Stop!* I told myself. God is looking after her.

I knew I wouldn't be able to eat or drink so I didn't order anything. I was sure I wouldn't be able to keep anything down. I pulled the tray down in front of me, folded my jacket in thirds and placed it on the table. I leaned my head down and closed my eyes, concentrating on not being sick.

I felt a hand on my arm and jerked up.

"You okay, child?"

Beside me sat a large, kind-looking woman with mahogany skin. Her black hair was pulled up in pins. I looked into her gentle eyes. "I'm okay," I said, but tears threatened and I couldn't stop them. I grabbed a balled-up Kleenex from my bag and dabbed.

"That doesn't look okay to me." Her voice was like silk. "You're shivering," she said.

"I guess."

"Well no wonder you're shivering, you've got that air nozzle aiming right smack dab down on you. Here, let me help." She reached up and turned the little blower off. "But I expect that's not the whole reason you're shivering, now is it?"

I shook my head, but I knew if I said one word, my eyes would gush over and I would not be able to stop this crying. And I didn't want to cry in front of a stranger.

Her hand was still on my arm. "Would you mind if I prayed for you?"

I looked at her in surprise and nodded vigorously. "Oh please, yes, do. That's exactly what I need."

And so she did, quietly, no louder than a whisper. She prayed that whatever the situation was, that I would know that God loved me unconditionally, just the way I was, and that God would intervene. *How could she know that this was just what I needed to hear?*

I felt a little better after that. Perhaps there was a pinpoint of hope. When I found my voice I said, "I've done some awful things in my life. And if I'd spoken up sooner, terrible things wouldn't have happened."

"Jesus forgives the most awful of things."

All I could do was to shake my head.

"I even used to think I was called by God," I muttered quietly. I didn't think she had heard.

She surprised me by saying, "We've no greater calling than to worship our Lord."

We talked that way, quietly between ourselves, all the way to Boston. She spoke to me about God's love, and how whatever it was, God would provide me with answers. Just when I needed them, they would be there.

Right before we landed, I whispered to her, "I was wondering, could you continue to pray after we land? Like in the next few hours? Everything is happening now, and I hope I'm not too late."

She patted my arm and said, "You will remain in my prayers for a long time, child. And you're not too late. I know you're not."

We exited the aircraft. As I gathered my bags from the overhead bin, I lost sight of her. I wanted to find her again, get her name, thank her. Out in the terminal I looked for her, but she was gone.

Because that kind woman was praying, I was sure that Bridget would be there and all would be well. The whole totally bizarre idea of Mrs. Eberline, dead and buried in her backyard, would be laughable. We'd go there and Mrs. Eberline's grandson would really be her grandson, and he would really be tearing up the deck to put a new one in, and Mrs. Eberline would really be on a cruise.

But when I got to arrivals, Bridget was not there. My heart sank. I waited. I tried her cell. No answer. I hung up without leaving a message.

I considered calling Greg or Paige, but realized that by the time they got here, I could already be home. A cab would be exorbitantly expensive but what choice did I have? Making the connections on the T would be painfully slow, and I needed to get there now.

I hailed a cab and again called Paige. I got no answer and I left a message. I called Greg and left a message asking him to meet me in the front of my apartment and to call me as soon as possible. I pocketed my phone. Fortunately the cab driver said not a word all the way through the city, which was good. I didn't feel like any small talk tonight. My heart was in my throat all the way home.

It was dark by the time I got to my apartment. I paid the cabby the equivalent of my life savings and he drove off. A figure came toward me from the steps of my apartment. I backed away into the streetlight.

"Lilly?"

"G-Greg?" I stammered. "You scared me half to death. I didn't see your car."

"It's in the shop. Getting the brakes fixed." His good hand was stuffed in his pocket. He still had the splint on, but the sling was gone. He touched my hair and then enfolded me into a one-armed hug, saying, "How was New Orleans? And what's all this about Bridget?"

"She's gone. She's disappeared. And I don't know where she is." I glanced up at our third-floor windows. "It's all dark up there. I'm so worried."

"She's probably on her way to get you right now. Did you try her cell?"

"She's not answering. I know something's wrong, Greg. She's at Mrs. Eberline's and she's in danger. We have to go there."

I gave him the condensed version of what happened as I pulled him around the side of my building toward the backyard, still dragging my carryon behind me. I stumbled on a root and Greg caught me. "Careful, Greg, I don't want you hurting your arm."

"Lilly! Wait." His grasp on my shoulder was tight. "Why don't we do the obvious first? Let's check your apartment."

I put my hand to my forehead. Was I letting my imagination run away with me?

"You're shivering," he said, taking both of my hands in his good one.

I broke away from him. "We have to go to Mrs. Eberline's!"

"Bridget is fine, Lilly," Greg said, taking my bag. "That story you've just told me about bodies in the garden sounds like Hitchcock or something. I'm sure Bridget is napping in her room, and that she's going to be mortified that she forgot to pick you up. At least let's go up and drop off your suitcase."

"I guess you're right," I said. "I'm just not thinking straight."

"It's okay, babe," he said with unexpected gentleness. I stopped, tears welling in my eyes. After all I'd said and done, he was calling me babe? "I'm sure your neighbor is fine, too. It's that all of this, everything you've been through, has made you fearful, and for good reason. And then there's me. I've just not been as understanding as I could've been."

My breath caught in my throat. He was apologizing to me? I was the one who needed to apologize to him.

As Greg brought my carry-on up the three flights to my apartment, I asked him what happened to his car.

"It was the weirdest thing. I was driving out in the country, which was a good thing, and I hit the brakes for a stop sign but the car just kept on going. I pumped and pumped the brakes, but they just weren't there. The road was straight and slightly uphill; I managed to come to a stop by gearing down. I'd had trouble with the brakes before, but nothing like that. So I got it towed to the shop."

"Greg!" I said, horrified. "It could have been so much worse! What if you were on the highway?"

"Well, thank the Lord I wasn't."

I unlocked the door and opened it cautiously.

"Bridget!" I called as we entered the dark apartment. No answer. I turned on the lights. There was a full pot of coffee waiting. Our automatic coffeepot had turned itself off. I touched it. It was cold. It wasn't like Bridget to make a pot and then forget it. And she hadn't put the coffee can back in the refrigerator. That definitely was not like her.

"Maybe she's on her way to pick you up and your wires got crossed. Maybe she got the time wrong."

"Not Bridget," I countered. "She never gets anything wrong. She's the most organized person I know."

I knocked on her bedroom door. When there was no answer, I opened the door a crack and called into the darkness, "Bridget?" Nothing. I turned on her light and her room came to life. There was her canopied bed with the pink frills, her doll collection lining her book-shelves, her stuffed animals each with their own special story. I always kid Bridget about her ruffles. She is so classy and chic in the outside world yet her bedroom looks like Barbie's dream house.

I opened up the white antique secretary where she kept all her important papers. I found her cell phone. Turned off. "That explains why she isn't answering her phone," I said, showing it to Greg. "She isn't on her way to pick me up. She never goes anywhere without her cell phone. She's very safety conscious."

"I'm sure there's a simple explanation."

We made our way into the main room. "I'm going over to Mrs. Eberline's now." I grabbed my keys and went down the three flights of stairs and back out into the cold night air.

I raced around my building and into the strip of yard between the apartments. I pulled up the piece of chain link and scooted underneath it. Greg was breathless behind me.

"Tell me again why you think she's at the neighbor's house?"

I expanded on the story I'd told him earlier, telling him about Neil and the flyers and the envelope in the courier bag. Greg followed me as I scrambled over roots and leaves in the yard. I was heading toward the back deck at Mrs. Eberline's. Maybe we could get in that way.

We had to climb over a four-foot brick wall which circumscribed her small, square deck. The dirt around the deck was a mess, and the flowerbeds were still torn up. The cloth chairs on her deck were covered with dust and grime, and several flowerpots had been overturned. I thought of the short, sturdy woman who'd coming barging into my apartment with a cake tin and I knew she would never leave her place like this. Cruise or no cruise, she would make sure it was kept clean. It also didn't exactly look as if anyone was working on any deck renovation.

The back door was locked. I had the feeling that this particular door had multiple deadbolts and chain locks on the inside. However, next to the door was a window with a four-inch space where the curtains didn't quite meet in the middle. I tried to peer inside, but all I could see was blackness. I banged on the window and called, "Bridget! Mrs. Eberline!" No answer.

Greg was examining the dirt piles. I shuddered to think about what they could signify. "Let's go around front," I said. "Maybe we can get in that way."

We climbed back over the brick wall and went around to the front. Even though we were surrounded by buildings with thousands of people inside, it felt to me as if we were out on an ice floe, miles from anyone, vulnerable and alone. My right hand was cold and my left hand was warm. I hadn't even realized that Greg had taken my hand. Maybe I wasn't so alone on the iceberg after all. I felt more than heard a slight movement to my left. I turned, but saw nothing in the blackness. Maybe an animal?

At the bottom of the apartment building's stone steps, Greg asked, "We couldn't get in the back. What makes you think we'll get in here?"

"I don't know. But we have to. Bridget could be there. And it's all my fault,"

"How is it your fault?" he asked.

"I should have paid attention. I'm not very good to my friends," I said.

Greg held me back by tightening his grip on my hand. "Lilly, please stop selling yourself short. You're a great person and a great friend."

I looked into his eyes. He was serious.

"Greg...I'm...we have to find Bridget." I twisted

out of his grasp and ran up the steps. Greg followed. I was surprised to discover that the door had been propped open with a rock. Maybe one of the apartment dwellers was out for a quick errand and didn't want to be bothered with a key on his return. Wasn't that how Mrs. Eberline had gotten into my apartment?

I examined the buzzer box to check the apartment number and then walked down the hall to her door. I knocked and called. Nothing. Then Greg tried the door, and the knob easily moved in his hand.

"Unlocked," he said.

Something was very, very wrong here.

I entered tentatively behind Greg, his hand holding mine. A faint light glowed from the kitchen. Greg flicked on the light switch and flooded the room with brightness. I gasped. I turned. Another intake of breath. Another turn. Another gasp. I turned and swirled until I was spinning crazily in the room. Every inch of wall space was covered in Lilith Java Band posters and pictures of me. Even the awful photos that Moira and I had been forced to pose for were here. I closed my eyes. How could this be? I was mortified, deeply humiliated. This was a side of me that even Greg couldn't imagine. This was the part I'd left out of my story, the part he couldn't know about, the part which could put an end to his love for me. This was the deal breaker. I moved away from him. I couldn't look at his face.

On a coffee table was a pile of the flyers that had been put on the windshields, plus a handful of CDs. Greg picked one of these up, studied it and said, "We need to call the police."

"Right. The police." I avoided Greg's eyes, not knowing where to look.

He said, "I should have called 911 right away when you called from the airport." He extracted his phone from his pocket and dialed.

I really didn't want the police here. I didn't want anyone to see all of this. I wanted to race through the place, tearing down the posters the way I had torn all the flyers off the cars in the lot. I didn't. I knew this was a crime scene and the police would need to see it intact, no matter how mortified I was by it.

Most of Mrs. Eberline's furniture had been moved against the wall and piled in a heap, chairs on her couch, end tables on the chairs. Even Mrs. Eberline's bedroom had not escaped. Her bed was shoved up against the wall, the dresser on top of it to make room for Lilith Java paraphernalia.

I looked toward the hall in the kitchen and jumped. A woman was standing there. But as I moved closer I realized that the apparition was just my black leather costume tacked up on a wall, with boots resting on the floor.

As I wandered through the main room and into the small kitchen, careful to not touch anything, I heard Greg on the phone quietly explaining what we'd found. There were more pictures on the wall in the kitchen. These were snapshots, small three-by-fives tacked up evenly all over the wall, edge to edge. I saw pictures of Moira and me, of Jason, of Mudd, of Mudd and me. So many, I had no idea there were so many. Where had all these come from?

There was only one answer. Mudd. And in the eight years I'd been away, his obsession had reached a terrifying level.

Mudd's sleeping bag lay flat on the floor against one wall. The neatness of it surprised me, the way the edges of it aligned perfectly with the wall. This gave me a niggling feeling, something that I sensed I should remember, but the feeling left me just as quickly as it came.

On a small table beside the sliding glass doors was a set of binoculars. I looked out the window and could see my own apartment just across the yard. I knew if I picked up the binoculars and placed them to my eyes, I would see into our apartment. Mudd had a clear view of our kitchen. He could see everything. He could see us plugging in our kettle. He could see us making toast, reaching for plates, talking on the phone. I remembered the rose and the card, and shuddered.

I stood in the center of the kitchen. Greg was still on the phone. The plates and saucers were piled neatly, small plates on top of larger ones. The floor was perfectly swept. On the kitchen table was the unsigned recording deal, the one I'd walked away from. I looked at it. Not millions, but a decent six-figures. Was this why he was stalking me? Because I'd run away from the record deal?

There was a church bulletin on the counter next to the stove. I grabbed it and opened it. My name was there as leading worship, and Mudd had circled it with a red marking pen, along with Paige's, and interesting enough, Stuart's. I don't know why, but I folded and pocketed it.

As I passed the small bathroom, I felt another shock. My old guitar—the one I thought I'd lost, the one my father had given me—was leaning against the tub.

I rushed toward it. Lovingly, I bent to pick it up, but as I did so, I recoiled in horror. A long knife had been stabbed into the back, and pierced through the front. That was the last straw for me. I slumped onto the cold bathroom floor and rocked back and forth, moaning.

Greg came and knelt beside me. There was pain in his eyes. I knew he didn't know quite what to say. Wordlessly he opened his arms and I went to him. "Oh, Greg, I'm sorry. I'm so sorry. This is the part of my life I didn't want you to know about. This is the part of me I didn't want anyone to know about. Not now. Not ever." My eyes filled with tears. How could Greg continue to hold me, to stay with me, when he'd seen those pictures? I tried to break away from his tight grasp, but he wouldn't let me go. He just held me tighter.

"None of this matters. None of it does. I love you just the way you are. I always have. I always will. Nothing will change that ever."

I leaned away just enough to look at his face. I tried to remember the last time he had told me he loved me. It was the day I got the first e-mail. "But—"

"No buts, babe. That's the way it is, and that's the way it always will be." Smiling, he wiped my tears with the fingers of his right hand. "So get used to it. The police are on their way. We're supposed to go to your apartment and wait for them there."

"Good," I said. "I want to get out of here."

He helped me up. But we didn't get to leave Mrs.

Eberline's apartment. The officers arrived just as we were emerging from the bathroom. I could barely look at them as they stared, astounded, at the hundreds and hundreds of photos of me.

SEVENTEEN

One of the officers who sat with us in the kitchen was Roy, the same cop with the rubbery features who'd come to the church when I'd been trapped in the basement. The other cop introduced himself as Rael. When he talked I could see a mouth full of uneven teeth. He crossed one thin leg over the other, took out a small notebook and placed it on his knee.

I mostly sat there, my head bowed, staring into my lap. Greg sat close beside me, holding my hands in his. He wouldn't let go. But I still couldn't look in his eyes.

Quietly, I told my story again and again, beginning with seeing the dirt in Mrs. Eberline's backyard and ending with Neil's phoning me with her address. I left nothing out. I talked about my basement ordeal, although Roy already knew about it, and I also told them about my trip to New Orleans to tell Moira about the $60,000. It took me a long time to get it all out. I was young. I was stupid. Mudd's nickname for me, Loser, kept crawling its way into my head. *Greg, I'm nothing but a loser. Why are you sitting here with me and holding my hands like I'm someone you could love?*

They got up and went out to the deck. While Rael checked out the piles of dirt, Roy got out a cell phone.

"We have some more officers coming," he told me after he finished his call.

"What about Bridget?" I asked.

"Are you absolutely sure she's just not visiting friends or out of town?"

I nodded, and so did Greg. "We're sure," Greg said. "Please listen to Lilly. What she says is the truth. If she says that Michael Binderson is alive, you need to believe her."

Roy was shaking his head. "Folks, Michael Binderson is dead. He died eight years ago in that shoot-out in New Orleans. He was positively identified."

I spun on them. "Everyone thinks he's dead, but no one knows for sure. No one actually saw his body."

"Ms. Johnson," Roy said gently, "his body was identified by his mother."

"His mother was a drunk. She couldn't even take care of her own family." I couldn't keep the panic out of my voice, but I needed to continue. "Several people have positively identified Mudd alive, here in Boston. I could get their names for you if you want."

Greg got up and went to the window. "Officers," he said, "the person in jail for Binderson's murder has always maintained his innocence. He claims he was knocked out, and when he woke up the gun was in his hand. He doesn't remember seeing Binderson's body."

Rael quipped, "Jails are full of innocent people. Everybody in jail says they're innocent."

Unconsciously I was fingering the bulletin in my pocket, the bulletin I'd grabbed from the kitchen counter. I took it out and put it on my lap. I was folding a corner of it back and forth and back and forth. It gave me something to do with my hands.

They had more questions for me, and I answered them as best I could. When did I first notice the mound of dirt in the garden? Did I see anyone? They were interested in the guitar and they put on latex gloves to examine it.

They asked me what Bridget had said on the phone and I played the message for them. I went through story again and again until I felt wrung out and tired. But I got the feeling that they might be beginning to believe that Mudd was alive.

A little later, Paige arrived. "I got your message," she said, sitting down right next to me and hugging me. She said, "They'll find Bridget. This will all be over soon."

Paige broke away from me and went over to Roy. "Is it absolutely necessary that these pictures stay up here? There's no reason why they have to remain up."

I heard them talk quietly. I saw the determined slant of her jaw, her hands on her hips. After several minutes, she turned off the lights in the living room. She came over and put her hand on my knee. "He said we couldn't take the pictures down, but we could turn out the lights."

I thanked her. The snapshots on the kitchen walls weren't so bad—I didn't need to turn out the light.

But something was bothering me—something was not quite right. I couldn't put my finger on it. I was shredding the edges of the bulletin, trying to figure it out.

I glanced over at the orderly arrangement of Mudd's sleeping bag, the edges touching the wall just so with not a wrinkle, the rectangular pillow precisely in the middle. I looked at the counter, at the dishes washed and put away one on top of the other, smaller stacked on larger. The place was spotless.

Something clicked then, like a finely tooled piece of machinery slipping perfectly into place.

In New Orleans, Mudd did not wash dishes. Dishes were left in the last place he'd been eating, sometimes staying there for days collecting insects until Jason picked the plates up and washed them. I remembered the basement in that house. His clothes lay where he stepped out of them. His sleeping bag was always in a crumpled heap. And writing love notes and sending cards with flowers—even to stalk someone—were not Mudd's style. Mudd couldn't identify a rose if his life depended on it. If he didn't like something, he said it outright. Mudd would not wait eight years to get revenge.

And then I knew. Mudd *was* dead. He'd been dead for eight years, just like I'd been told. They had been right and I had simply failed to see it.

I huddled myself into my remembering, while Roy went around the apartment taking pictures and writing notes. And while he did this and they talked among themselves and made calls on their cell phones, I thought about a young boy, nicknamed Psychopath by his older brother, Mudd. I thought about a younger brother I never knew by name. I remembered him sitting on the edge of the couch, quietly, unobtrusively, staring at me with his large eyes through the glasses he wore, even then. He followed me around, all the time, until Moira would say, "You have a secret admirer."

We would come home from gigs and there he would be, patiently working through chords on my acoustic guitar. And he would look lost and hurt when I would tear it out of his hands and say, "Don't ever touch my things again!"

"Why not, Lilith Java? Why not?" And he would skulk away. The next day he would follow me around saying, "Teach me, Lilith Java, teach me how to play like you do." His eyes would follow me as I walked away. Eventually, a social worker would come and take him away, but he'd be back. He never stayed more than a couple of months in any one house. "Kid's a psychopath," Mudd would say. "That's why."

I remembered a solemn younger brother who listened at doorways when we sat around the table discussing band business and upcoming gigs.

I remembered a younger brother who had a camera. Why had I not remembered that until now? I remembered a younger brother who would know all about the sixty thousand dollars, a younger brother who would guess what I had done.

I was putting it together now. *You could always marry me.* What I had heard as lighthearted humor from a classmate who I considered my own little brother, was in fact, something more. When I had asked him to put together that CD, I had offered him my flash drive of songs. But he already had them on his hard drive. Why would he have kept my songs on his computer?

It was Neil. It wasn't Mudd who was obsessed with me now. It was his brother, Neil.

I remembered seeing Neil putting flyers on the windshields. He'd told me that he'd gone back to the cafeteria to try to return the courier bag to the guy who'd asked him to do it. But that's not the way it was, was it? I could picture him throwing that bag into his car and then driving off. Why hadn't I seen the signs? His overt neatness, his always seeming to be at the same place I was.

But what about the pork-pie hat? Easy. He got it from his mother. Neil, who idolized his older brother Michael, must have saved everything of Mudd's. And they were close enough in height and body build to be mistaken for each other.

I flattened the bulletin on the table in front of me and said, "I'm sorry. You're right. You were right all along. Everyone was. Mudd is dead. I know that now. But I know who did this. I know who's behind this."

Rael looked up sharply from his notebook.

"It's Neil," I said, placing my hands on either side of the bulletin and staring down at it.

Rael said, "Who's Neil?" at the same time that Paige said, "Neil from your school?"

I nodded. "He's Mudd's younger brother. I remember him…" I felt a cold shiver coming on. Paige sat very close to me. "He must have found my picture on the church Web site before I even knew it was up there and followed me to Boston. I'm sure of it." And as the five of us sat in the kitchen surrounded by Lilith Java Band memorabilia, I told them everything I knew about Neil.

"Is he after the money, do you suppose?" Greg asked.

I shook my head. "I don't know. I don't think so." I shoved my hair behind my ears. "He was always rather strange."

Rael was thoughtfully chewing on his pen while I talked. A new thought snaked its way into my head. I nearly gasped. Neil had given me this address. He *intended* to lead us here. He knew I would come. Did he know I would bring Greg? Possibly. We all heard a noise outside and I looked out the window to the deck, through the space where the curtains didn't quite meet. Someone was there. I felt it.

"Something's wrong," I said.

At that instant, the quiet was burst apart by shattering glass. A bottle landed on the floor. It looked like a Coke bottle, no, a large wine bottle, and it had a flaming rag stuffed into its neck.

We all jumped and yelled at once. Rael threw something on the bottle—his jacket, maybe?

"Back!" he yelled. He raised one arm as a shield and with the other he reached for his gun. As he approached the window, another bottle was thrown in. It broke as it hit the floor and the flames spread. The smoke detector began its earsplitting blast. I looked up at the space between the curtains and saw his face.

Mudd! I stared at him. But in the next instant I knew it wasn't Mudd after all. I could see it was Neil now. Neil without his glasses—he looked exactly like Mudd.

How had I not seen this before? His eyes locked on mine for one moment and he mouthed one word: "Lil."

The police fought the flames with a fire extinguisher and seemed to be winning. Paige, Greg and I were now firmly in the living room, away from the kitchen. I heard yelling outside and then someone said, "Turn around! Slowly! Hands up!"

The other officers had arrived in time to see what was going on. Through the shattered kitchen window, I could see the backyard suddenly fill with light. I wrenched myself out of Greg's grasp and dashed quickly into the kitchen, through the commotion, through the back door and out onto the deck toward Neil, doubled-over and handcuffed. The police inside were too busy trying to subdue him to pay much attention to me.

I heard someone reading the Miranda rights.

I stared at him. I felt as if I were in a trance, unable to speak.

He turned toward me and his face twisted in rage.

"You and me!" he yelled above the din. "We could have had so much, Lilith Java. We could have had so much."

I looked at his face and suddenly saw the little boy who followed me around, who even slept in my bed one time until I got home late after a gig and kicked him out.

"That money," he yelled in my direction, "that was our money to start a new life!"

"Where's Bridget?" I asked, approaching him.

"Miss," said a police officer, putting out his arm to stop me. "Can you back away please?"

"Where's Bridget?" I demanded.

"I was in the van that morning," Neil said. "I was hiding in the back. I followed you both in. I knew what was going down—I heard my brother on the phone. When Mudd knocked the other guy unconscious, I got the guy's gun and I killed Mudd! He wasn't treating you well. You needed someone like me who would take care of you. But when I came out, you were gone. And then when I finally found you, you were engaged to some loser boyfriend. I tried to do something about that, too!"

I knew it. Neil had been responsible for the removal of the floorboards and for Greg's brakes. I felt like I'd been hit.

But he still wasn't telling me what I had to know. I had to know where Bridget was. A police officer pulled me away but I yelled over his arm, "Where's Bridget? What did you do with her?"

He sneered and blew me a kiss. This was not the sweet Neil I knew from school, the young man who was like a little brother to me. This was a savage Neil, a Neil with fire in his eyes, a Neil I didn't know at all.

Suddenly Greg was there. "Lilly, Lilly," he said. "Come on back. Get away from him."

By now the officers had forced Neil into the backseat of the patrol car.

Greg pulled me back and I melted into his arms, shaking. When I looked up, I realized the whole yard was full of neighbors in nightgowns and pajamas.

"Will someone *please* shut up that smoke detector?" a voice yelled.

I was cold and shivering. Greg, Paige and I went over and leaned against the chain link fence that divided my yard from Mrs. Eberline's. Even though they told me I could go warm up in my apartment, I couldn't leave. Not with Bridget still in danger.

Floodlights were being set up around the deck, and officers began digging. I felt nauseous. What if Neil had killed Bridget? Could she be buried there? I couldn't stop shivering.

Rael came and told us that the police were searching the entire apartment complex for Bridget and that the apartments near the fire had been evacuated. Teams of police were swarming the area, some on phones. The entire backyard was lit up, and all the apartment windows, too.

I felt so tired as I sagged against the fence.

"It's all my fault," I kept saying. "I betrayed my best friend."

"You betrayed no one," Paige said. "None of this is your fault. You just get that notion out of your head."

"It's not your fault," Greg said. "Nothing that happened then or now is your fault."

I knew he was talking about the pictures and the money, and not going back after I heard the shots, and leaving Moira. But I didn't think I would ever forgive myself—I felt, down deep, that it *was* my fault. Nothing Greg or Paige—or anyone—said would make any difference.

I put my hands in my pockets. Somehow the church bulletin was still there. I pulled it out and looked down at the cover. The front of our bulletin always has a picture of our majestic church building. I looked over and saw it now, the spire standing proudly in the night sky. I thought about what Neil had said, about how easy it was to get in and out of a church. And it dawned on me. "She's at the church. That's where she is."

Greg gazed at me for a long minute before he went and spoke with a cluster of police officers. I saw him give them some keys. A few took off. He came back and told me they would look. We waited. We waited some more. I still would not go up to my apartment despite their many persistent urgings. I couldn't be in that apartment without Bridget. I shivered. I prayed. I thought about the lady on the plane. I knew she was praying, too.

A while later, an officer approached us. "They found Bridget. She was tied to a chair in the church basement. She's anxious to see you."

I collapsed in a heap on the ground and sobbed tears of gratitude.

When I looked up, I saw two officers holding up an exhausted Bridget, who could barely walk. But when she saw me, her eyes lit up and she broke away from them, rushing forward on her own.

"Lilly!" she called. "They said you told the police where I was! Lilly, you saved my life!"

We hugged and I couldn't stop crying. "I'm so sorry," I said, over and over again. And I was. All of this was my fault. All of it.

EPILOGUE

Later that night, they found Mrs. Eberline's body in the garden. An officer called to tell me. He also said Neil had talked all the way to the police station, mostly about me and how I'd betrayed him by leaving that day. He said he'd vowed to find me. We belonged together, he'd screamed at the top of his lungs. We were supposed to make music together and be famous, he kept telling the police.

It was Neil who'd lured me into the basement of the church. During one of our study sessions, he'd stolen my apartment key just long enough to get a copy made. For the life of me, I couldn't remember it going missing. He'd stolen Bridget's CD player knowing that it would be traced to me causing the police to doubt me. He'd also managed to send a message to me which looked like it originated from Paige's cell phone. I still don't know how he pulled that off. Neither do the police.

What did he hope to gain by all of this? That wasn't entirely clear. But I kept thinking that Mudd used to call him a psychopath. He was a troubled kid from a troubled family who grew up to be a troubled adult. He admitted to killing his brother because Mudd was not treating me well. Neil decided he'd be my savior and treat me so much better than Mudd did. He'd been looking for me for eight years and when he found me, I was practically engaged. That infuriated him to the point of madness. He wanted to kill Greg and frighten me into submission. Needless to say, the Mark Pelsar case is being reopened in New Orleans and it's expected he'll be released soon.

The day after Neil was arrested, my parents flew out from Iowa to be with me. There were new lines on my mother's forehead that hadn't been there three years ago, and my father looked older, too. I realized I needed to keep in touch more. They stayed in my room, while I slept on an air mattress in the living room. My mother didn't want to do this—she wanted to stay in a hotel— but oddly, Bridget convinced her to stay with us.

"This is family," I heard her say to my mother. "And she may not admit it, but Lilly needs you right now."

That was so like Bridget. She was the one who'd been kidnapped and tied up in the church, yet she was calling this entire thing "Lilly's ordeal."

It was a bit of a tight squeeze with all of us using one bathroom, but we managed. And in a way, it was nice, the four of us talking late into the night or playing dominoes on our kitchen table. One of the first things Bridget did after Neil was arrested was buy new curtains for the kitchen which, in a way, I sort of regret, since now we have a Barbie kitchen.

Tiff and Lora were shocked, as was everyone in

school. Tiff, who considered Neil a good friend, was epecially hurt. Neil had used her like he had used everyone else.

On the night before my parents left, my mother said to me, "We shouldn't be so estranged. Families should see each other, you know."

I knew this was her way of telling me that she loved me.

Despite the fact that things were normal now, and that Greg knew everything and still wanted us to be together, I made the decision to leave Boston. I wasn't running away this time. I was making a well-thought-out and prayed-over decision. I didn't think I'd ever get over the guilt of Mrs. Eberline's death and I needed a new start. Almost everyone understood why I felt it was time for me to leave. I think a lot of people even respected my decision.

Bridget didn't, of course. She didn't want me to go and she argued with me every time she saw me, which was every day. When I was at home in the apartment, she would try to get me to change my mind.

I would say, "Bridget, you almost died because of me. Mrs. Eberline *did* die."

She would shake her auburn hair and say, "No, it was your quick thinking that actually saved me. You're a hero! You figured out where I was. And you didn't murder Mrs. Eberline, Neil did."

Someone like Bridget would never be able to understand the guilt I felt. When you carry guilt for so long, it just doesn't disappear in an instant. It becomes a part of you, like your eye color or your shoe size.

"I need a fresh start," I told her. "My mind's made up. I'll be going to California. I've even found a school where I can transfer my credits."

"And you think going to California is the answer?"

I shrugged. We'd had this conversation many times.

"And what about Greg?" she demanded.

I sighed, closed my eyes. *What about Greg?* He still felt we had a future. We had long, long talks. We talked like never before. He told me more about his wife, and how angry he was with God when she died. But despite what he said, despite his assurances that he loved me, and that I was a good person, I felt that things would never be the same between us. How does anyone live down a life like the one I'd had? Sometimes I would even joke about it. "Well," I would say, "I guess I can never run for public office."

"Lilly. Please. You're not that person anymore. God knows it. I know it. And I love you."

I realized that I hadn't told Greg I loved him, not since before this whole thing began. I guess I just couldn't get the words out.

I had no other choice but to leave—it couldn't be helped. We were from two different worlds. In time he would get over me and find a nice wife from Bible school, someone who hadn't been forced into posing nude to make it in the music business.

I hadn't told Greg the exact day I was going. Maybe I was afraid. Maybe I didn't want to talk about it anymore. Maybe I really didn't want to leave.

Greg and I were on a winter walk along the seawall one night. It was cold and there was ice in the wind. I held my hair off my face as we stood on the wall facing each other.

He said, "You have a funny look on your face." His hands were in his pockets and he was staring down at me rather intently. We weren't touching.

"I'm leaving for California in the morning." I said it simply and quickly.

"You mean tomorrow?"

"Yes."

"And you're telling me tonight?" There was pain in his eyes as he looked away from me out at the sea.

A chunk of my hair blew in front of my face, and I brushed it away.

"What do I have to do to get you to stay?" he asked.

"Nothing."

Along the horizon out on the water a freighter made its way across the bay. Of course this wasn't the way I wanted it, but it was the way it had to be.

"Can I at least get a goodbye hug?"

I went to him and we held each other for a long time while the sea wind blew at our faces.

The following day I packed my car to leave before noon. It was raining and sleeting. Bridget tried to persuade me one more time to stay, but I kept saying no.

"At least stay another day, to avoid the storm."

"I can't. And I'm driving into clear weather anyway. I'll be careful."

We hugged, cried and promised to keep in touch. I knew we would. I would not betray another friend.

As I drove away from my neighborhood, the rain intensified. My windshield wipers could not keep up with the onslaught. California would be nice, I thought. They didn't have weather like this. I could even now picture myself sitting at an outdoor café drinking bowl-sized cups of milky coffee in the afternoon sunshine, writing in my journal.

But did I really want that, to be alone for the rest of my life, sipping lattes in a café like some tragic figure in a Kafka novel?

It's what I deserve, I thought as my front tires skidded across a wet spot. When I got out on the highway it was bad, worse than I expected. *I should turn back,* I thought. *No, I can't go back.* I'll just go for as long as I can and then get a motel. Or I'll sleep in the car along the highway until the rain ends.

I'd gone about forty miles when I began humming the worship song I'd taught to the church, the one I had written. I began to understand that I couldn't write the last verse simply because I had not lived it yet. It should be about God condemning sin, but also about Jesus, his son, taking that sin upon himself, taking that guilt, making all things new. And that it's only God who makes these new creatures. It's not something we can do on our own. The rain intensified, and I upped the windshield wiper setting to the highest again. Maybe what I'd been doing all along, I thought, was trying to become this "new creation" on my own. I'd turned my back on my past. I'd tried so hard to live the Christian life on my own, but it hadn't worked.

I was following a huge truck and getting bombarded

with his spray as well as the rain. I passed him, then moved my windshield setting down to medium. I thought about Greg and my eyes burned. During the past few weeks, Paige had told me that the Bible was not a rule book. "In fact," she'd said, "it has nothing to do with rules, except that it shows us that it's impossible for us to follow any rules, so in that sense, I guess you *could* call it a rule book."

Her words echoed in my brain on this wet, sleety day.

Maybe that was my problem. When I'd latched on to Christianity, I'd seen it as a new way to live. Good Christians prayed regularly. So that meant that to be a good Christian, I had to do the same. Good Christians went to church. So I did that. And because I was a singer—Paige even called me a hymn composer—I had some respect in the church. It was just a natural thing that I would marry the youth pastor. I was receiving special favor from God. And I loved my music. One of the things I thanked God for every day was that he'd called me to be a musician.

But maybe that's where I'd gone wrong. Paige had told me that I'd been called to be a musician. As I drove down the highway, though, I remembered what the woman in the plane had told me. "We have no other calling than to worship God."

Music had always been my life. It was the thing I did better than anything else. It's what I'd lived for since I was old enough to realize that if I opened my mouth, I could sing. Even when I was a part of the Lilith Java Band, it was what I lived for. And it was still what I lived for now. Nothing was different.

All I'd really done was to trade rock music for Christian music. Maybe even Paige had been wrong in this. Maybe the woman on the plane was right. My only calling was to worship God, not music. The idea startled me a bit, but it felt right.

There was a rest area up ahead. I was hungry and I needed gas. I'd pull off, and maybe grab a burger and a coffee to warm up. I had many driving days ahead of me.

I bought a burger and a coffee and found a booth where I could see my car. Some of my stuff was on a roof rack and I wanted to keep an eye on it. It had started to pour again. It was like a solid sheet of water cascading down the side of the building, undelineated by individual drops.

Lost in thought, I took a bite from my burger and looked up.

A very drenched Greg was sitting right across from me. I nearly choked on my hamburger. I opened my mouth to say something but clamped it shut again when no words came. I managed a kind of a strangled, "Wha…?"

"I know," he said. "What am I doing here? Well, I called Bridget. She told me when you left and what highway you were taking. So I took a chance and came after you. I had to." He ran a hand through his wet hair. I continued to stare at him without speaking.

"I've been tailing you since Boston, Lilly, wondering when you were going to pull over. I thought you'd've seen me behind you."

In that instant, I realized I didn't want to live my life without Greg.

"Lilly, I can't let you go. I really and truly can't let

you go. Will you come back so we can try again? We can make it different this time. Will you come home?"

It took me less than a second to say, "Yes, Greg, let's go home."

"You might want to bring this with you," he said, smiling.

Taking my left hand, he slipped on the most perfect diamond ring.

* * * * *

Dear Reader,

In *Shadows in the Mirror,* (Oct. '07) the first in my SHADOWS series, the main character, Marylee, didn't know anything about her past. That's not the case in this second book in the series, *Shadows at the Window.* Lilly Johnson knows her past all too well, and it's one she'd rather forget. In fact, she has gone to great lengths to make sure no one finds out anything about her. She has done just about everything but change her name. Even her fiancé doesn't know her real story.

After a fairly wild life, she came to faith in God. She read the Bible verse in 2 Corinthians 5:17, "Therefore, if anyone is in Christ, he is a new creation; the old has gone, the new has come!" and understood it to mean that if she worked hard enough to deny her past, she could become this "new creation" in Christ all on her own.

What she didn't know is that this is impossible. She needed to make peace with her past before she could come to grace and love in the present.

I think that most of us can identify with Lilly, at least a little. We may not have lived the life Lilly lived, but maybe we've done things we're not particularly proud of. I know I have. It's easy to hide these things, to pretend they never happened. What is difficult is coming to grips with them, asking forgiveness and then moving on. I, personally, take great comfort in the fact that God forgives me. All he asks is that I worship him and put him first.

I hope you enjoy *Shadows at the Window.*

I love to hear from my readers. I would be thrilled

to hear your story of becoming a "new creation in Christ." You can contact me at Linda@writerhall.com.

I also invite you to my Web site: http://writerhall.com where you can sign up for my newsletter and a chance to win an autographed book.

Linda Hall

QUESTIONS FOR DISCUSSION

1. Is there anything in your past that you're not particularly proud of? What have you done about it?

2. It could be argued that, right from the start, Lilly made wrong decisions. In your opinion, what was the very first mistake she made?

3. If you were in Lilly's shoes, what would you have done?

4. What exactly does the Bible mean when it says, "Therefore, if anyone is in Christ, he is a new creation; the old has gone the new has come!" (Corinthians 5:17) Does it mean what Lilly thought it meant, that when one becomes new in Christ, the old should be swept under the carpet and forgotten?

5. What is the difference between accepting your past and trying to hide it?

6. Lilly was told that her calling was that of a church musician. But the woman on the plane told her something different. What was Lilly's real calling? What is your real calling?

7. Lilly doesn't have a close relationship with her parents. Is there anything Lilly could have done to

change this? Are there family members that you feel estranged from? What are some tangible things you can do to change this?

8. Lilly was afraid that if Greg knew everything there was to know about her he would leave her. Do you think he would have? Would you have, if you were Greg?

9. Greg has his own past to deal with. Do you think he had completely dealt with the death of his wife before he met Lilly?

10. Would you have been as forgiving of Lilly as Moira was?

11. By her own admission, Lilly says she "tries hard to live by the precepts of the Bible." What was wrong about this thinking?

12. Which character in *Shadows at the Window* did you most identify with, and why?

13. Who was your favorite character in the book and why?

REQUEST YOUR FREE BOOKS!

2 FREE RIVETING INSPIRATIONAL NOVELS
PLUS 2 FREE MYSTERY GIFTS

Love Inspired
SUSPENSE

YES! Please send me 2 FREE Love Inspired® Suspense novels and my 2 FREE mystery gifts (gifts are worth about $10). After receiving them, if I don't wish to receive any more books, I can return the shipping statement marked "cancel". If I don't cancel, I will receive 4 brand-new novels every month and be billed just $4.24 per book in the U.S. or $4.74 per book in Canada, plus 25¢ shipping and handling per book and applicable taxes, if any*. That's a savings of over 20% off the cover price! I understand that accepting the 2 free books and gifts places me under no obligation to buy anything. I can always return a shipment and cancel at any time. Even if I never buy another book, the two free books and gifts are mine to keep forever.

123 IDN ERXX 323 IDN ERXM

Name _____ (PLEASE PRINT) _____

Address _____ Apt. # _____

City _____ State/Prov. _____ Zip/Postal Code _____

Signature (if under 18, a parent or guardian must sign)

Order online at www.LoveInspiredSuspense.com
Or mail to Steeple Hill Reader Service:
IN U.S.A.: P.O. Box 1867, Buffalo, NY 14240-1867
IN CANADA: P.O. Box 609, Fort Erie, Ontario L2A 5X3

Not valid to current subscribers of Love Inspired Suspense books.

Want to try two free books from another series?
Call 1-800-873-8635 or visit www.morefreebooks.com

* Terms and prices subject to change without notice. N.Y. residents add applicable sales tax. Canadian residents will be charged applicable provincial taxes and GST. Offer not valid in Quebec. This offer is limited to one order per household. All orders subject to approval. Credit or debit balances in a customer's account(s) may be offset by any other outstanding balance owed by or to the customer. Please allow 4 to 6 weeks for delivery. Offer available while quantities last.

Your Privacy: Steeple Hill Books is committed to protecting your privacy. Our Privacy Policy is available online at www.SteepleHill.com or upon request from the Reader Service. From time to time we make our lists of customers available to reputable third parties who may have a product or service of interest to you. If you would prefer we not share your name and address, please check here. ☐

LISUS08R

Love Inspired® SUSPENSE

TITLES AVAILABLE NEXT MONTH

Don't miss these four stories in August

THE GUARDIAN'S MISSION by Shirlee McCoy
The Sinclair Brothers
Heartbroken after a failed engagement, Martha Gabler
heads to her family's cabin for some time alone. But her
retreat soon turns deadly. With gunrunners threatening
her life, Martha has to trust undercover ATF agent
Tristan Sinclair to protect her—and heal her heart.

HIDDEN DECEPTION by Leann Harris
Elena Segura Jackson is frightened when she stumbles
upon her employee murdered, and she's terrified when
the killer starts vandalizing her shop. Clearly, she has
something the killer wants...but what is it? With Detective
Daniel Stillwater's help, can she find it in time to save
her life?

HER ONLY PROTECTOR by Lisa Mondello
All bounty hunter Gil Waite wants is to find a fugitive and
collect the reward. Then he meets the fugitive's beautiful
sister. Trapped in Colombia while rescuing her brother's
baby, Sonia Montgomery needs Gil on her side if she's ever
going to get herself and her niece safely home.

RIVER OF SECRETS by Lynette Eason
Amy Graham fled to Brazil to atone for her family's sins—
she never expected to discover Micah McKnight, the man
her mother betrayed. Micah doesn't remember who he is,
and Amy is too scared to tell him...but as danger escalates,
Amy's secrets could cost her everything.

LISCNM0708